SEE
THROUGH

STORIES

NELLY REIFLER

SIMON & SCHUSTER
New York   London   Toronto   Sydney   Singapore

I am deeply grateful to the friends and teachers who read these stories throughout various phases of development and helped shape them with criticism and interpretation: Elizabeth Albert, Hilary Bell, Astrid Cravens, James Gibbons, David Hollander, Siri Hustvedt, Dylan Nolfi, David Ryan, Brooke Stevens, Gina Zucker, Mary LaChapelle, Joan Silber, Linsey Abrams, and Lucy Rosenthal. More thanks go to the fine people of Darhansoff, Verrill, Feldman, especially Kristin Lang, and most of all Leigh Feldman, my frighteningly smart agent. Still more thanks go to David Rosenthal, Tara Parsons, and Victoria Meyer at Simon & Schuster—and I feel especially lucky to have worked on this book with Marysue Rucci, my wise editor. I appreciate the support given to me by the Rotunda Gallery in Brooklyn and the Henfield Foundation. And I thank my dear boss Mr. Paul.

SIMON & SCHUSTER
Rockefeller Center
1230 Avenue of the Americas
New York, NY 10020

Some of these stories were previously published as follows: "Rascal" in the *Florida Review*; "Personal Foundations of Self-forming Through Auto-identification with Otherness" in *Bomb*; "Teeny" at Failbetter.com; "Memoir" in *Ducky.com* and in the *Saint Ann's Review*; "Sugar" in *Post Road*; "See Through" in *Black Book*; "Julian" in the anthology *Lost Tribe: Jewish Fiction from the Edge* (HarperCollins).

For information about special discounts for bulk purchases, please contact Simon & Schuster Special Sales: 1-800-456-6798 or business@simonandschuster.com
Manufactured in the United States of America

1 3 5 7 9 10 8 6 4 2

Library of Congress Cataloging-in-Publication Data

Reifler, Nelly.
See through : stories / Nelly Reifler.
p.   cm.
I. Title.
PS3618.E555S44 2003
813'.6—dc21
2003050379

ISBN 0-7432-3608-4

For my parents,
Ellen Marshall
and
Samuel Reifler

and
also
for
Josh Dorman

CONTENTS

TEENY   1

BABY   11

RASCAL   17

JULIAN   31

MEMOIR   41

THE SPLINTER   49

UPSTREAM   63

THE RIVER AND UNA   81

NORTH CURVE   93

PERSONAL FOUNDATIONS OF
   SELF-FORMING THROUGH AUTO-
   IDENTIFICATION WITH OTHERNESS   99

SUMMER JOB   109

SUGAR   117

AUDITOR   125

SEE THROUGH   141

SEE
THROUGH

TEENY

There they were.

Through the window, she could see them, one on either arm of the sofa.

They seemed to be asleep.

She had her instructions, written on a piece of lined notebook paper. She had reviewed them earlier. Now the paper was cinched in her fist, blank side out, words hidden. Her hand was sweaty.

She looked at them through the window.

She leaned forward and pressed her free hand against the glass. Her breath made a spot, which disappeared instantly from its edges inward.

What were they doing? Were they sleeping? Were they just lying there with their eyes closed? Were they dreaming? Were they thinking?

The key to the house dangled from a plastic lanyard, which she had snapped around her belt loop when she got dressed that morning.

Her fist tightened. The instructions crinkled.

It was just yesterday that she had been inside the house with her mother. Yesterday the people had shown her the plastic bowls on the kitchen floor. The litter box in the laundry room. The emergency numbers on the refrigerator. She had knelt on the kitchen floor and patted the striped one on its head, and her mother had said to the people, "See? She's a natural. She'll probably be a vet when she grows up." It was yesterday, yes, but it seemed so long ago. In her memory, yesterday's visit was a slow blur, as if her eyelashes had been glued together. Now, again, looking through the window, she felt as if she were peering through a thicket of eyelashes and glue.

She backed away from the window. Slowly, slowly, away from the house. She stumbled on a low green wire fence which guarded a flower bed. She almost fell, but she caught herself. There were no flowers there yet; it was too early. There was just dark brown earth, which had recently been turned over, and a few tiny green sprouts.

At the bottom of the driveway, she looked up and down the street. No one was around. No one saw her.

That evening, she lay on the living room carpet with a stack of chocolate chip cookies on her belly. She ate them slowly, contemplatively. She had started out with six, but somehow she had only one cookie left when she heard her mother's car in the driveway. There was the grinding noise of the garage door. Silence for a moment—then the click of the car door opening, and a thump when it closed. She shut her eyes and put a placid

expression on her face. She rested her arms by her sides and let her legs flop open.

The door between the garage and kitchen opened. She heard keys drop on the table. Water running.

"Teeny?" her mother called.

She lay still.

"I need some help here, Teeny. Where are you?"

She heard her mother's voice come closer. Her legs felt like wobbly gelatin. Her stomach turned over. Her heart started beating faster.

"What are you doing? Are you sleeping?"

She didn't answer. She felt her hands clench into fists, then let go, once again weak and droopy.

There were footsteps. She felt her mother's breath on her forehead.

"Are you okay, hon?"

She didn't answer.

"So, did you go? Did you do it? Was everything okay?"

She opened her eyes and looked at her mother. A pendant with a cameo locket hung around her mother's neck and dangled down, swinging in a small arc. There had been a baby picture inside, but her mother had taken it out. She said she was waiting for the new grown-up school photos to arrive. They were due any day.

"I was thinking today," said her mother, "you could really make this into a regular job. Everyone has pets, and there are no other children the right age on this street. Bill, Heather, Candy, Lakshmi—they're all too old, when you think about it. They have regular after-school jobs and wouldn't want to take anything else on. Brandon, Jason, those twins at the corner— they're too little to handle something like this. I'm sure that the Stines will recommend you to everyone once they see what a good job you've done."

She closed her eyes.

The next day, she dawdled on the way home from the bus stop. She walked up and down the aisles of the card shop. She opened a card that sang happy birthday in a whiny electronic voice. She tried out a highlighter pen. Then she sat on the curb outside the grocery store and watched cars come and go. By the time she got to the house, it was late afternoon, almost evening. The windows reflected the white sky, and the sun was the color of a dusty nickel.

She cupped her hands around her face and looked in at the living room.

First she saw just one, scratching at the sofa, then it darted out of sight, and then both were there, running around, chasing each other, paddling at each other's faces with their paws.

She stood there, suddenly frozen. Moving only her eyes, she looked over at the front door.

She reached for the lanyard on her belt loop. It was woven from flat vinyl string. She remembered the long crafts hall of Camp Sacajawea; she remembered the sound of rain pounding on its zinc roof the day they learned to make lanyards. She remem-

bered how some of the girls had made wallets, and burned their names into the leather with a glowing hot tool. But the counselors hadn't offered to teach her how to make a wallet. Why? Why had they only given her the vinyl string? She had lain in her bunk that night, wondering how the counselors decided who was ready to make wallets. Did they know something she didn't know for sure but suspected?—that she wasn't capable of using that burning tool? How did they know that about her? Could anyone know it just from looking at her? She had wondered if her mother would notice, at the end of the summer, that she had come back with a lanyard and not a wallet. She had wondered: What would she tell her mother if her mother asked about it? That they didn't have enough leather to go around, and she hadn't wanted a wallet anyway. Or that, instead of making a wallet, she had taught a younger camper to braid the colored vinyl.

Now she let go of the lanyard. She wiped her damp hands on her corduroys, and pulled her shirt down over her belly. Looking through the window again, she saw that they were still at it, bouncing around, hiding from each other, pouncing, rolling around under the coffee table. Sweat trickled from her temple, past her ear, down her cheek. She could feel the blood rush into her head, then flow away, then pour into her skull once again.

She turned and hurried to the end of the driveway, pausing to look up and down the street.

That night she sat on the floor, picking red gummy worms out of a waxy paper sack. Her eyes were half closed; she tried to open them all the way, but the lids just dropped back down. A couple of hours earlier, her mother had walked in, throwing her tote bag full of papers and clipboards on a chair, then rolling her knee-highs down to her ankles. "I'm sorry I'm late," her mother had said. "I was training the new agent on the com-

puter." Her mother asked if she had eaten, and she shrugged. Her mother asked if she had done her homework, and she made a gesture toward a textbook open on the table. Then her mother asked how her job went. That was when it had become necessary to walk over to the closet and get the candy bag from her jacket pocket.

Now all the red worms were gone. She sat there with her empty hand in the bag. Her mother was on the phone in the kitchen, and her mother's voice faded in and out like a faraway station on a car radio. From under her lids, she looked down at her torso, the alien bulges and folds of flesh that spilled out around her waistband, her junior bra under her T-shirt. She curled forward, folding her arms around her head, blocking out the electric light. She could smell the new smells of her armpits and crotch in the dark little room formed by her concave body. She wished she could live in a space like that; it would be quiet, and she would be the only inhabitant.

The next day, after school, she sat on one of the benches next to the gazebo in the courtyard of the shopping center. She was rereading her favorite Goosebumps book. Every few minutes, she looked around. She worried that her mother might show up. She had a story ready. She would say the science teacher was sick and she got out of school early, so she had already gone and done the feeding. She would say that she ran into Lakshmi and Mrs. Krivalli, and they had taken her to do some shopping. She would say that Mrs. Krivalli suddenly wasn't feeling well, and she had to go to the doctor. So she was sitting here, waiting to see how Mrs. Krivalli was.

But her mother did not appear. It started to get chilly. She folded down the corner of the page she was on and headed slowly back to her street. She didn't mean to, but on the way home she stopped and looked in through the windows. Inside,

they were sitting, pressed up next to each other, eyes wide open. When she shifted forward—just the littlest bit—they both noticed her. They stared straight at her. She watched them open their mouths. They hopped off the sofa and ran over near the window. Her heart flooded, then contracted. She took a tiny step backward. They were looking at her, mouths opening and closing. Their eyes were wild and hopeful and pleading. She could only imagine the noises they were making. Looking at their mouths opening and closing, she could almost hear them saying her name. "Teeny," they were saying, "Teeny, Teeny, Teeny. . . ."

She backed away from the window. The sky had turned gray. She felt a raindrop. She was about to leave when she noticed that a pile of newspapers had built up near the front door. She opened the outer screen door, which the people kept unlocked, and she shoved the papers inside the shallow entryway. There was a pair of yellow plastic clogs there, and a green umbrella. She grabbed the umbrella and pulled her jacket close to her body. It used to zip; in fact, last spring it had been loose, but now she had to hold it closed with her hand.

In her room, before bed that night, she unrolled the loose-leaf paper where the couple's instructions were written in the wife's loose, cursive hand. The wife was beautiful, and wore a masculine haircut and glasses which made the curves under her clothing impossible not to stare at. The day she got the job, she had noticed how the wife's flesh had bobbed and undulated under her big shirt. The man was friendly. He had a little beard. They had given her the phone number of their hotel. She could call them, she thought, she could tell them everything. She stared at the slanting letters, the long loops and low bumps. She saw the words "handful dry food"; she saw the word "water." Her stomach clenched. She rolled the paper into a tight ball and threw it under her bed. She took the green umbrella hanging

from her chair and shoved it under the bed. Finally, she grabbed the lanyard from her desk and threw it under there, too. She heard the key hit the floor.

She turned off the light. In the dark, she pinched her nipples hard, and they gathered and wrinkled. She kept going until they were sore.

She didn't stop at the house the next day. She walked the long route home from the bus stop, along the gas pipeline where the weeds were soft and pale. She stared at the tips of her tennis shoes, pushing their way through the grass like little animals. She imagined she wasn't moving her feet; they were just snuffling along on their own.

The next day was Saturday. The couple was supposed to come home on Sunday. At breakfast, her mother said, "I just want you to know how proud of you I am. You're a big girl now; you've done your first job. Have you figured out how you're going to spend your money?"

She shrugged.

"You can't spend it on candy, remember, that was a condition of taking the job. And you can't spend it on Goosebumps books, it has to be a real book. And you can't spend it on candy."

She pulled her shirt down over her belly.

Later, she stood outside the house, but she didn't look in the windows. She was tempted, but she didn't let herself. She could remember how their voices had sounded in her head, calling her name. She shoved the latest newspapers inside the vestibule. As she was leaving, she stopped at the bottom of the driveway. In

just a few days, more sprouts had come up. Some had real leaves on them. She kneeled down and put her fingers around the smallest green stem. It was silky and moist. She pulled. The one hairy white root seemed to quiver in the air. She shuddered and threw the plant down on the dirt. They were going to come home the next afternoon, around one o'clock, they had said. She counted the number of hours between now and then on her fingers. The little hairs under her arms stood up and sweat soaked her shirt.

The next morning, she said she didn't want breakfast. Then, when her mother was in the laundry room, she climbed up onto a chair and got a box of chocolate chip cookies from the cabinet. She tucked the box under her arm and went upstairs to her room to wait. She read, trembling, until twelve-fifty-five, then put her book down.

It was another wet day. She could hear the rain in the aluminum gutter outside her window. She remembered the crafts hall at Camp Sacajawea. She remembered the hair of the other girls, how it seemed to hang just right from their heads. Their limbs had seemed to belong to their bodies. She remembered watching one girl, watching the long straight hair that fanned across the girl's shoulders as she leaned forward to etch her name in brown leather. "Eleanor," the wallet said. "Eleanor"— a name like a grown-up lady's, a name like a queen from a fairy book. The girl's arms had been slender; they stretched from the short sleeves of her T-shirt, looking like the firm branches of saplings. The girl's flat, golden stomach had shown above the jeans that hung off her hips.

She finished the box of cookies. It was one-oh-five. Five minutes later, she heard car doors down the street. Soon after that, she heard voices below her window. The doorbell rang, several

urgent rings in a row. She heard her mother trotting to answer it. The doorbell rang again. And again. And then the sound of the front door opening.

She put her arms around her head and curled forward into her dark space. She inhaled and wondered how long she could hold her breath.

BABY

The baby was smart. Too smart. He was also sickly.

When he was six months old, he started to speak. By nine months he could form complete sentences. "Mom," he'd say, lying on his back in the crib, dolphin mobile dangling overhead, "I feel unwell. I'm weary. There's some kind of sticky liquid in my lungs and it hurts to breathe." Or: "Mom, my diaper's full of diarrhea again. My stomach is cramping. I'm not absorbing nutrients properly. I'm dehydrated."

His mother was at her wit's end. She tried to get him to rattle his rattle. She tried to interest him in a magnetic choo-choo train. But he'd just groan and turn over on his side.

One brilliant day in autumn, she sat on the window seat in the nursery. It was warm in the room, and she leaned against the cold window. Sunlight flickered with the movement of leaves falling off the big oak in the yard. At the baby's request, a tape of Bartók played on the yellow Fisher-Price tape player. The baby lay on his back with his arms in the air. He studied his fingers, squinting.

"Mom," he said in his reedy little voice. He paused, wheezing. He was having asthma, and she was keeping watch, ready with the inhaler.

"Yes?" she said.

"Mom, we all die, right?"

She sighed and looked out the window. A squirrel circled the base of the oak. Red and yellow leaves fluttered in the air. The squirrel picked up an acorn in its little paws.

"Mom?"

"Yes," she said, "that's right."

"Well," said the baby, still looking at his fingers, "if everyone dies, what's the point? I mean, why should I try so hard? What does it matter if I breathe or not?" He wheezed.

She watched the squirrel dash off, around the side of the house. "Because you'll grow up to be a great person," she said. "You'll do important things. You'll have friends. You'll travel."

"I know," said the baby. "But in the big picture, in the whole scheme of things, it doesn't really matter, does it? Someone else would come along and do what I would have done. The friends I might make would never know the difference if I didn't exist. The world, the universe—I'm just a speck, really," the baby said. He made fists, then rotated his arms. "The Bach cello pieces are on the other side of that tape, right, Mom?" he said. "Could you flip it over?"

His mother walked over to the tape player on its little red painted table. She remembered seeing the table in a store window one day when she was pregnant. She remembered going into the store and paying for the table. She remembered carrying it into the hush vacuum of the nursery.

Now she turned the tape over. She picked up a plush yellow duck from under the table and brought it over to the crib. She made it dance a little, then tucked it under the baby's blue flannel blanket.

"Oh," said the baby, wheezing, "this is the tape with that bad Dutch cellist. Could you find the other, please? With Yo-Yo Ma?"

The mother reached into her pocket. She produced the inhaler and leaned into the crib. She stroked the baby's fine yellow hair. She traced his white eyebrows with her finger.

She brushed away the granules of dried gunk from the corners of his eyes.

"My baby," she whispered. She brought the inhaler to his mouth. He opened wide, she squirted, he inhaled.

"Tastes like burning plastic," said the baby, wrinkling his nose.

The mother watched him breathe for a second, then went back to the window seat.

One day, early in her third trimester, she had met a friend for lunch in town after an appointment with her obstetrician. The printout from her sonogram was in a manila envelope inside her purse. As she eased herself out of her car and walked to the café, she found herself stroking and caressing the envelope. She reminded herself not to talk too much about her baby. She reminded herself that her friend, recently divorced and childless, was having a tough time and needed her attention. But after half an hour of hearing about the friend's disappointments and struggles, she couldn't help herself. She pulled the envelope out of her purse and handed the fuzzy, black and white image across the table. Her friend took a swig of wine and squinted at it. Then she laughed.

"What's so funny?" asked the pregnant woman.

"See his hands? It looks like he's saying something in sign language." Years earlier, the friend had dropped out of audiology school to get married.

"And what would that be?"

"Well . . . ," the friend giggled, raising her right thumb, and supporting her right hand with her left. "See? It looks like he's saying 'help.'"

The mother-to-be tried to laugh, but a chill began to crawl up her body, from the soles of her feet and across the hairs of her thighs to her crotch, where she felt a fluttering tremor. When she got home that day, she went straight upstairs to the nursery and lay down on the floor in the blue late afternoon light, both hands resting on the mound which housed her baby. She had sensed him moving, shifting incessantly, like an insom-

niac tossing and turning, never finding the right position.

Now she heard the baby clearing his throat. "Ahem," the baby said. "Mom?"

She opened her eyes. She hadn't realized that she had shut them.

"Mom, what about my question? What's the point?"

His mother said nothing. She looked out the window. There was the squirrel again, circling the oak again. But was it the same squirrel? She couldn't tell. All squirrels looked the same to her.

"Mom," said the baby, "Mom. My bronchi are clearing. Mom," he continued, "I said I didn't want to hear this. I said I wanted Yo-Yo Ma."

The mother groaned. She stood up, walked over to the tape player, turned it off. She unzipped the nylon case where the baby's cassettes were stored, dragged her finger along the plastic tape cases, then pulled one out, opened it, and put the tape in the player. She pressed play.

"Thanks, Mom, I really appreciate it," said the baby. The mother went back to the window seat. She looked out the window. No squirrel. A breeze passed over the lawn, and the leaves rose and swirled.

"But Mom," said the baby, "Mom, are you there? Mom, are you paying attention? What do you think? What's the answer? Why do we do it? Why do we continue, knowing all the while that life is finite? Why do people brush their teeth, go to work, eat, laugh, if they're just going to wind up things, cold flesh, food for the maggots?"

His mother watched out the window. Suddenly, two squirrels came into view, from opposite directions. So there were two of them all along, she thought. One squirrel leapt onto the tree and started to climb. The second squirrel followed. Was it chasing the first, she wondered, were they courting? Were they competing for acorns?

"Hello? Mom?" said the baby. "Hello, Mom. Are you there?"

"I'm here," said the mother. "What do you need?"

"Do you believe in God?" asked the baby. "Do you think there really is a God, or is religion just something that human beings have created to cope with the fact that their lives mean nothing?"

The mother heard the neighbor's teenage daughter pull out of the driveway in her Honda; its broken muffler coughed and rattled.

The mother stood up and walked over to the baby. She looked down at him again. His fingernails were tiny, like bits of sea glass. His skin was so thin and translucent, she could see the blue veins clearly, branching out from his arms to his hands to his fingers.

"My diaper is wet," stated the baby.

The baby had shoved his pillow to the side, and the mother picked it up, intending to put it back under his delicate skull. But then she found she had the pillow in both hands. She found herself leaning forward over the baby. She saw her hands lowering the pillow; she saw the pillow covering his face. She felt herself pressing down, hard, pressing the pillow against his nose and mouth. His arms twitched. His little fists beat against the sheet.

On tape, the bow met the cello's strings, the bow danced with the cello.

An acorn knocked against the window.

The mother jumped back from the baby. She threw the pillow on the ground.

She kicked it into the corner.

The blue paper dolphins floated over the crib.

The mother stared down at the baby. He was still. His eyes were closed.

She started to lean forward into the crib again.

Then his eyes opened. The baby opened his eyes and looked up at his mother. He looked at his mother's face. He looked into her eyes. He did not blink. Ever so slightly, he shook his head, side to side.

He said nothing. He was nine months old.

He would wait.

RASCAL

Hunter. Airborne. Wildfire. Slingshot.

Intense. Boulder. Giant. Dagger.

In the end, Robby chose a Dagger bike, because of the name. *Dagger*. He remembers that when he first saw the silver logo on the bike's shiny black frame, he imagined splitting the wind on it, stabbing up hills, ripping around curves.

Now, lying in his sleeping bag, he catalogs all the good things about getting around on his Dagger. For one thing, it's cheap. No gas. You never pay a toll, and you can usually get away with camping for free. And another thing, you never get stuck in traffic. Even if there's a traffic jam, you can just dart between the cars. Slicing like a dagger. He likes to grin into the rolled-up windows of cars that are moving about a yard an hour. *Screw you,* he thinks as he pedals past. By the time he's rolling a fresh joint in Dolores Park, they're finally leaving the city limits of San Jose.

So what if he doesn't have his own car anymore? Robby kneads his thigh muscles. They are rock-hard and knotted. These bulging forms that push against his skin are as impressive as his 'Stang ever was. He is lucky. His life has order. He's in shape, and he doesn't spend that much time with his mom and dad.

It is a bright night. The moon is big and low over Andrew Molera State Park. His nylon shorts hang on a string between two branches of a live oak. Every evening, he heats up water over a fire, washes his face with a small bar of Cashmere Bouquet, and then dips his shorts in the leftover soapy water. A rinse in the spigot, then he wrings them out and strings them up. It's part of traveling light.

Most every night, there's someone to talk to wherever he's camping. There were those bikers last summer coming back from Sturgis. They showed him their new tattoos and their customized Harleys. They offered him beer, which he declined. They were cool with that. The bikers had already laughed and patted him on the back when he told them the whole story— how he'd been arrested and had his license permanently revoked for too many DUI citations; how he had a hot girl-friend, a nineteen-year-old hippie girl with long hair and silver toe rings who lived in the Haight. He passed around a pipe, and they told a story about a guy with a Japanese bike at Sturgis. A "rice burner" they called it, an ugly thing shaped like a cockroach, with purple streaks and lots of white plastic. Fast and quiet as hell, but light, bad in the mud. The guy won a lot of races. But so what?—said the bikers—Guy wins the races and heads back to the motel the last night of the rally. He's rounding a blind spot on a little hill, and a truck pulls out of a tavern, kills the guy on the spot.

"Loud pipes save lives," said the biggest, oldest biker. Robby felt uneasy for a second. After all, Robby was the other kind of biker, a cyclist, really. But at least his bike was American.

Robby smiles when he thinks about how he impressed the bikers, even though he hadn't told them the real story. The truth was, he didn't have his license taken away for good, only for two months—he could apply for a new one any time he wanted. And there was no girlfriend, never had been. Somehow, he couldn't tell the bikers how simple his life was. Making this loop from Mom and Dad's to Dolores Park is his job, and

he's his own boss. When he first lost his license, the plan was slightly different. He thought he'd bike up to S.F., buy a big bag of weed. He thought he'd sell it to rich Bakersfield kids at a nice profit. But as it turned out, the weed was really good, and he found himself taking the long route back, camping out and getting stoned. The little monthly allowance from when his grandmother kicked it is just enough for an ounce of marijuana. He never sells it, just rides back and forth, smoking it. He rests for a couple of weeks a month, hanging out in his room with the bong, or playfully bickering at the kitchen table with his mom. After his arrest, he promised her he'd never drink beer again.

He must still look like a beer drinker, he thinks proudly. People always offer. On the way back from San Francisco last month, he met an old man at one of those fancy campgrounds where half the sites have cement rectangles for parking RV's. The old man was going to visit his grandchildren. His RV had carnival lights strung beneath the awning—not the colorful ones you usually see, but yellow with black silhouettes of naked girls, like on the mud flaps of an eighteen-wheeler. The old man assumed Robby was a serious athlete in training. Who else would refuse a Heineken? Who else would ride from Bakersfield to San Francisco on a bicycle? When Robby said he didn't drink beer, the man poured some Gatorade in a glass and pointed to the roof of his RV. There was a tiny satellite dish up there. The man told Robby he'd been following the Tour de France and Lance Armstrong on ESPN. "Even with no nuts," the old man said, "that fella's more man than all those Krauts and Dagos put together."

"What's a Dago?" Robby asked.

"You know, kiddo, an Italian."

"I thought Italian guys were Wops," said Robby.

"Either one, my friend," said the old man, grinning. "They're all mama's boys."

Robby felt nauseous for a second, and he looked down at the

ice cubes floating in his Day-Glo green drink. When he looked back up, the man was still smiling. His dentures gleamed in the lamplight. He raised his beer and said, "God bless you, kid—you've got what it takes. You're Armstrong with both balls." He clinked the can against Robby's glass, and Robby nodded, smiling back at him.

Tonight, the campground is pretty empty. It is a Tuesday night. He arrived early this afternoon. First he found a site far away from the ranger station, then he rode around and around the park, looking for someone to talk to. He avoids families, and this afternoon the only people around were families. The dads acted meek, as if they were nothing more than chauffeurs hired to drive minivans, and the moms were as stiff as sergeants in their white tennis shoes and their windbreakers. The little girls were shrill; you could hear their voices bounce off the earth. The little boys were either like sad stunted men or they were menacing, running around with sticks and rocks. He does not want to have any contact with children. He is always sure they will nail him in some way, say something true and mean that he does not want to hear.

So this evening he gave up on meeting anyone. He steamed a microwave burrito from a 7-Eleven by propping it with sticks over a pot of water. While his burrito defrosted, he went into the trees and smoked half a joint. The live oaks were so low, the top of his head poked through the upper leaves. It was the last of this ounce; he smoked with end-of-the-bag urgency. Then he lifted the hot burrito using the twigs as chopsticks. He smiled at his ingenuity. He opened the purple plastic wrapper. He wondered why plastic does not melt when it's steamed, and he thought about how his mom had soups that came in little plastic pouches. You put a pouch in hot water, then slit it open with a knife. In grade school, he recalled, there was something called Career Day, and a lady from the Sausage Makers' Union came with a filmstrip that showed a pig's bladder being slit open. Liquid flowed out like soup. Did they use the bladder for

sausage? Robby could not remember. But thinking about it made him have to pee. He ducked into the grove again, sniffing his hands before he reached into his shorts.

The Heet Mistake had happened last fall. Returning home exhausted at the end of a trip, he'd lost control as he rounded the last corner onto his mom and dad's street. He hit the Puctneys' mailbox and went flying over his handlebars. He landed on his shoulder in the gravel driveway. He lay there, just looking at all the sharp gray stones and wondering what had happened, until Mrs. Puctney came running out of the house. He sat in her kitchen, scraped up and sore, until his mother came to get him. Instead of going right home, they went to the drugstore. Robby waited in the car, and his mother came out with a bag of supplies: the largest Band-Aids he had ever seen, extra hydrogen peroxide, a quart of strawberry ice cream, and a tube of something called Heet. That evening, while he was eating ice cream and watching TV, his mother rubbed the Heet on his shoulder. It really did feel hot, and Robby inspected the aluminum tube, amazed that it was room temperature.

When his mother went out to get Robby's pizza, his shoulder started throbbing again, and he decided to rub some more Heet on it. He squeezed a blob of it out on his hands, rubbed them together, and massaged himself as best he could. Then he had to go to the bathroom. As soon as he reached into his fly, he realized he had made a mistake. He yelped from the pain once, then pulled his pants off and jumped into the bathtub. When his mother came home, he was still soaking in ice-cold water, tears drying on his face. Ever since, he always smells his hands before taking a leak.

As he watered the live oaks, he thought again about what an important lesson he had learned from the Heet Mistake, and he renewed his pledge to write a letter to the company as soon as he got home. He zipped up, grabbed his burrito, and began his stroll around the campground in his bare feet. While he walked, he planned what he would say in the letter. "Dear Heet," he

would start, "do you know how dangerous your product is?" His mother could type the letter for him.

It was growing dark. The families had built fires in their pits. Smells of hamburgers and franks came from every direction. He couldn't figure out what would come next in his letter, but smelling the cooking meat made his burrito even more enjoyable, and he chewed it slowly.

Then, as he neared his site again, he noticed that someone had come in while he was gone. A tent was pitched two sites away from his. A small Japanese car was parked between the tent and the drive. There was no evidence of children. Robby stepped into the soft dirt circle of the site. He leaned against the little red car and crumpled the purple burrito wrapper with one hand. A female voice came from inside the locust-shaped blue tent.

"Love?"

"Yeah?" A male voice came from the trees. A young guy emerged. He noticed Robby and said, "Hey."

Robby was not sure if this "hey" was an exclamation or a greeting. From the way the guy nodded and curled his lips, Robby decided it was a greeting. The guy had messy blond hair tucked behind his ears. He wore a T-shirt with a picture of a coffee mug on it. Steam rose from the mug up to the crew neck; underneath the mug, in slanted letters, was the word "Ah!"

There was movement in the tent, then the sound of a zipper. A foot in a purple sneaker poked out of the tent. It was the same purple as his burrito wrapper, Robby observed. Soon, Robby learned that the foot was attached to a red-haired girl, Sharon. The guy was Dave. They were from Maryland.

He learned these things when they were all sitting on the ground near the fire circle. Sharon had taken some blue corn chips from the trunk of the car. They ate these chips as they got to know each other. Robby was so relieved that they had shown up at Andrew Molera, and he told them so. He was imagining getting them high and making them laugh at his sto-

ries of road life. He told them how he felt about families, how all dads have fallen arches, and moms have steel-toed Reeboks for kicking the dads. Sharon nodded. Dave looked at her and squeezed her hand.

"What's your family like, then?" said Sharon.

Suddenly, Robby felt something rise from his toes to his jaw that made him stiff and hot. Did she think he was talking about his own mom and dad? He leaned forward to her, looking in her eyes, and said, "My folks are perfect. My mom . . . she bakes these snickerdoodle things"—he giggled, because the name of those cookies always makes him giggle—"and Dad . . ." He thought about how to explain Dad. "He goes back to Delaware every August to do a Revolutionary War reenactment." In his mind, Robby saw his dad—well, a photo of him—in the red jacket, holding a musket. Robby's older brother, Fred, who worked in the faucet business with Dad, had started going to Delaware each year, too. The photo in Robby's mind was actually a picture of the two of them, on a hill with an old fort in the background. They had the same broad shoulders and barrel chests, and the same serious, squinting eyes. They wore white wigs and three-cornered hats. They hadn't invited Robby yet. Everyone in the family agreed it might not be his sort of activity, just as they agreed that faucets might not hold his interest. He and his mom had fun alone, anyway, playing canasta and watching Carol Burnett. He rarely saw Fred anymore. He had bought a condo and moved in with his girlfriend.

"Dad's a redcoat," Robby said. He decided not to mention Fred.

"That's cool," Dave said. "*My* dad made a documentary film about these Elks in Arizona who reenact battles of the Civil War in their backyards." Dave laughed. Robby felt muddled. Somehow, Dave hadn't understood how much it meant for a son to have a father as brave and as strong Robby's. Dave didn't understand the difference between the Revolution and the Civil War. The Revolution was about Liberty and Justice for all. The

Civil War was about . . . something else. Robby thought of his mother's videotape of *Gone With the Wind,* that dark maid lady, with the big white eyes. Then he remembered his discomfort riding through parts of San Jose at night, the shadowy people who threaten him by lurking—it seems like they wait for him. They know things about him, the routes he takes, that he's carrying weed. He sometimes imagines how his life might be simpler if the slaves had never been freed.

There was a silence.

Sharon said, "I really wish I'd known my dad." She leaned toward Dave. Then she explained to Robby, "He died when I was two. But sometimes I dream about him. I dream he comes to my bedside and watches over me."

Dave squeezed her hand. "We're on vacation, Shar, let's not . . ." Then he kissed her near her eye. He said, "My father and my stepmother and my mom all love you, Shar."

Sharon said to Robby, "My mother is an alcoholic. I'm not talking to her until she gets help. I'm tired of being my mother's mother."

Robby looked at the two of them. He hadn't made much of an impression on either one. They were a unit, like a pair of hands stroking and holding each other. He said, "Well, I'm camping right there." He tipped his head toward his site. "If you need anything, just yell." But even as he said it, he knew he sounded dumb. What could he offer them? They seemed to have everything.

Hours later, he can't fall asleep. For all his positive thinking, he has ended up back at Sharon and Dave. What a disappointing encounter. In all his trips back and forth, he's never met people so uninterested in him. He starts to feel angry. Sharon asked him about his family, but really she just wanted to tell him about hers.

He flexes his feet and feels the tendons stretch up the backs of his legs. He remembers stepping on the back of his big brother's head once when he was a little kid. His brother screamed. His mom came out on the deck. "Oh, my little ras-

cal." He remembers her laughing. "You just don't know your own strength." But he did know his strength. He could never concentrate on math or history, but he always knew how to twist someone's arm until they begged.

Robby remembers that visit to the school counselor after something had happened in the lunchroom involving a twisted arm. Robby was in seventh grade. He and his mother and the counselor guy, Fitzman, sat in an office on the same hall as the principal. Robby remembers Fitzman, his corduroy suit and his mustache. Robby's mom said to Fitzman, "Boys are tough with each other. My boys roughhouse day in and day out."

"This is more than roughhousing," Fitzman said. Robby had a rubber band ball along that he was squeezing. He'd started it with two little rubber bands his mom gave him from around Andy Boy broccoli. Now it was as big as a softball. Fitzman was not smiling. He said, "When I was a kid, sure, we kicked, punched, all that. But it was never so . . ." He turned to Robby. "When you feel yourself getting mad, just ask yourself, Am I going over the line?"

Robby looked down at the ball.

"Can you say that?" Fitzman asked.

Robby brought the ball to his nose and sniffed. It smelled like chalk and tires.

"Robby?" Fitzman said.

"What?" Robby answered.

"'Am I going over the line?'"

Robby mumbled something, "Emuh gung ovuhlie."

"Good boy!" his mother exclaimed, patting Robby's cheek, then mussing his hair. "See?" she said.

"I don't know," said Mr. Fitzman. "Can you try again?"

Robby felt his face turning red. He shook his head.

Fitzman sighed. "Well, it's a start, I guess," he said. "Maybe this'll change when he gets interested in girls."

"Girls!" His mom laughed. "He's just a boy—all that business is a long way down the road."

On the way home, Robby's mom had taken him for a milk shake, like when he'd had his rotten baby tooth pulled out by the dentist. He sucked on the vanilla malted, and she pressed his hand with hers.

That proves it, Robby thinks. People have always been interested in him, even busy, important people like Mr. Fitzman. He decides to give Sharon and Dave another chance to be impressed. All the families have gone to bed. He hears an occasional noise from the dying fires. Snap, Crackle, Pop, he thinks—but which was which? Three little elves, and he's never thought of it before, but they look just like that cookie elf who lives in a tree, and like the Lucky Charms leprechaun without a beard. He remembers his Smurf collection, and he imagines Grandpa Smurf sitting in a blue rocker on a blue rug by a blue fireplace, with his throat slit, spurting red blood.

He yawns.

Stretching his fingers and toes, he wishes he was hanging out with the bikers tonight. They were such a great bunch of guys. The night Robby met them, the big old one was working on his saddlebags, cutting strips from a tough, strangely shaped piece of leather and tying them around the buckles. His knife caught Robby's eye. It was long for a collapsible knife, about five inches, and shiny steel. On the side was etched "Schrade." When Robby got back to his mom and dad's house, he told his mom he wanted that kind of knife. But she came back from the army-navy store with one that said "Buck" on the side. He put it back in the shopping bag and sulked for days until she asked what was wrong. "No offense, Mom, but you're not a very good listener," Robby said, and pulled the knife out of the bag, pointing at the lettering on the blade. His mother wagged her finger at him, laughing. "Picky, picky boy," she said, but then she patted Robby's cheek and apologized. She took the knife and drove away. She returned with his Schrade. Now he carries it with him all the time. Just tonight, he used it to cut the twine for hanging

up his shorts, and also for opening the burrito wrapper. He keeps it in his sleeping bag for protection at night.

This knife would impress anyone. He'll go back to Sharon and Dave. He'll say, "Psst. Hi, guys." He imagines them poking their heads out of the tent, looking sleepy. Then he'll say, "It's a beautiful night. You've got to see the moon." They'll have a better conversation. He'll show them the Schrade and tell them the big biker gave it to him. He imagines them asking to hold it.

He slips out of the sleeping bag and takes his shorts off the line. They're still damp, but that's okay. He takes a hit off the roach from earlier. He feels the weight of the Schrade in his left hand. He walks through the trees in his bare feet. He comes out right beside Sharon and Dave's tent. He's about to say, "Hi, guys, it's me." But instead, he circles the tent. Once, twice. Then he is kneeling down at the fly. He listens for noise from inside the tent. He imagines they are having sex, right now, and he almost giggles. He hears nothing, though. He waits. Are they alive? After a moment, he hears Dave cough and move. The nylon of the sleeping bag scratches along the ripstop of the tent. It sounds like insect wings.

Slowly, Robby pulls at the zipper that keeps the fly taut. In the moonlight that shines through the side of the blue tent, he can see their hair, and some of Dave's face. Dave's hair is blue-blond, his skin is blue-pink. The nails of Sharon's hand that dangles off Dave's shoulder are blue-white.

Robby opens the Schrade, crouching at the maw of the tent. He's moving the knife slowly in the air, picturing the biker. Suddenly, he realizes the shape of the biker's piece of leather was the shape of an animal's back: neck, shoulders, rump. The biker's leather was the skin of an animal. He almost slaps his forehead in amazement. Of course he knew that leather came from animals, but he's never thought before of how it is skin, really skin. He doesn't slap himself, but he moves his heel and it scrapes a pebble.

In the tent, there is motion. Sharon's head turns and lifts toward him. He could still say "Hi," but nothing comes out.

Her eyes are open, looking at him. They are blue, with blue brows and lashes. She looks at him with a puzzled expression, then her eyes move down to the Schrade. They have a different look when they move back up to his face. She starts to open her mouth, but he smiles and puts his index and middle fingers to his lips. He feels cozy; he is recalling how his mom would visit his bedside while Fred slept. She would always do that, put her fingertips to her lips, before she stroked restless Robby's hair. He would fall asleep with her fingers on his scalp.

Robby moves his empty hand into the tent. It turns blue. Sharon's eyes look funny. Her eyebrows are all furrowed up, and she's not blinking as she looks into his eyes. He touches her hair with his hand. It's softer than it looks in its short, tomboy haircut. He moves the hand with the knife into the tent. The shiny steel shoots a beam of light right back out through the ripstop toward the moon. Robby smiles widely. It is a beautiful night. He lifts a small handful of Sharon's hair, some of her thick bangs. He slices through it with a swift, clean motion. She opens her mouth again; he hears a tiny squeak. He finds his hand moving the Schrade to her neck. His other hand holds her blue-red hair. He looks at her forehead, which is now exposed to the blue light. And across her forehead, he notices, is a line. Not a wrinkle but a wide, raised scar. It stretches diagonally from her part to the opposite brow. He can see that it cuts into her eyebrow; there is a hairless spot, pale and shiny. Robby has always been proud that he has not a single scar. All those cuts from roughhousing, and his skin sealed right back up every time. He moves the hand with the blade up to Sharon's forehead. Holding the handle with four fingers, Robby runs his pinkie along the waxy ridge of tissue. Then he thinks of his own body, his own skin like a rubber suit that holds his past inside.

Robby moves his hand away from her face, but his pinkie

still feels the smoothness of her scar. He eases his hand out of the tent. Then, carefully, softly, he edges backward on his haunches. He feels her watching him move away.

Back in his sleeping bag, he is still clutching Sharon's hair in his right hand. For a second, a question bobs to the surface: "Did I go over the line?" He brings the clump of hair to his nose and sniffs it—shampoo and bug spray. His stomach tightens, and he feels a little queasy. But then a TV set flashes on in his head, and he forgets everything else. He sees the Little Rascals. Alfalfa's pointy cowlick was like a horn, Robby thinks. He remembers the one when Alfalfa and Spanky went camping. Did Spanky and Alfalfa let their little brothers come on their trip? Of course not. But the kids followed the big boys all the way to the camp. Both pairs of boys pitched their tents and unrolled their sleeping bags. But when dinnertime came, Spanky and Alfalfa had forgotten their food.

The big boys sit there, looking at each other. They are close to tears. Alfalfa hits Spanky on the crown of his head. "Ow!" says Spanky, and he hits Alfalfa back. "Ow!" says Alfalfa, and he hits Spanky again. Nearby, the little ones eat bread and jam. But in the end, do they share it or keep it for themselves? Robby can't remember.

JULIAN

Julian balanced between the rungs of the cast-iron gate. He held the stationary fence and swung in a slow, small arc back and forth. The iron hinges squeaked. Rebecca rummaged in her purse for the keys. When she found them, she pushed open the front door, then turned and waited for Julian to get down from the gate.

Julian hopped down, then took a couple of uneven steps away from his mother and the front door, dragging his right foot behind him.

"Come on, time to go inside," said Rebecca.

"Today, in Yard," Julian said, "I learned to limp."

"Please, sweetie, you can play later," said Rebecca.

Julian's father, Herzl, had said he would try to make dinner. When Rebecca and Julian entered the house, there was no smell of food being cooked, no heat coming from the kitchen. Julian ran past his mother through the living room and back door, into the garden.

Herzl was in the hammock, curled up sideways, with his knees pulled up to his chest. One arm was hooked over his head, and the other covered his eyes. The ground around him

was stained black from the summer's mulberries. The hammock was big and stretchy, woven from bright green cotton string. Herzl's body weighed it down in the middle, so it supported him just above the ground and folded over him. Julian thought of a picture book they had at school about monarch butterflies, and the fields of jade-colored cocoons hanging off thousands of milkweed plants.

Julian dropped his knapsack and jacket on the ground and ran to his father. He pushed the hammock but could not move it. Julian's chest tightened. He pulled the taut ropes and looked at Herzl, then reached out a finger and poked him.

"Gentle . . ." whispered Rebecca behind him.

Herzl opened his eyes. Julian let out his breath and almost laughed. He waited for Herzl to smile or wink. He wanted his father to pull him onto the hammock, he wanted to get tangled in the stretchy webbing and fall onto his father's belly. But Herzl just looked at him; his eyes were the only part of his face that moved, and he looked Julian in the eye.

"Hi, Dad," Julian said. He made himself sound sullen and removed, like a teenager on TV.

"You didn't make dinner," said Rebecca. Then she added, "It's okay."

"I'll make dinner," said Julian. "I'm going to make dinner. I'm a good cook, Dad, right? I'll make omelets!"

"I'll make dinner," Rebecca said. Julian heard her close the door partway as she went inside the house.

Julian backed away from the hammock. His father pushed himself against the fabric and turned himself around. The hammock tipped, and he sat just inside its edge, crouching, feet on the ground. Julian could see how his father had changed: his skin did not fit his big bones, it hung slack on his chest and belly. The treatments had given him rashes and had made his hair patchy. Julian stared at his freckled scalp.

He reminded himself again of that time long ago, when he was just a little kid. Herzl had taken him upstate to the sculp-

ture park. He had been strong, and he had lifted Julian onto a couple of the giant metal monsters and taken pictures of him. Julian knew this had happened because one of these snapshots was framed on his grandmother's wall. On the way back into Brooklyn, they were stopped at a red light. Julian saw two figures in the doorway of a building. He pulled on Herzl's sleeve and pointed. A tall, thin man was bent over a tiny old lady, who was holding her pocketbook to her chest. "Wait here," Herzl said to Julian, and he pulled over and got out of the car. Julian pressed his face to the window and watched Herzl go and talk to the man; they seemed to argue. The woman backed away and opened the door with several keys. Julian was watching her when he heard shouting and saw someone run past the car. Then he didn't see his father, and then he realized Herzl was lying on the ground. Julian started screaming inside the car. He tried to open the doors, but Herzl had locked them all. Some people came over and were brushing Herzl off as he pushed himself up to sit on the sidewalk. Julian kept screaming. Herzl gave the keys to someone to let Julian out. He ran over to his father, who was talking with the people around him. Julian leapt at his father from behind and clutched onto his head. He buried his fingers in Herzl's pale, woolly hair. Julian hardly remembered the rest of the night. The important parts of that day, Julian reminded himself now, were that his dad had lifted him up and taken pictures of him; that his dad had saved a lady from being mugged; that his dad had been hurt but was okay, and had sat up all on his own.

Herzl was rubbing his hands together, and Julian could see the crisscross pattern of the strings on Herzl's arms. There was a sketch pad under the hammock. Next to it was Herzl's pen, which Julian loved to use. It was a special pen, a Rapidograph filled with India ink. Julian looked at the pad, but from where he stood, he could not make out the drawing on the page. It was small and dark and seemed to be quite detailed. He squatted to get a closer look, but Herzl reached down and closed the

pad. Julian felt himself blush. He thought he had seen wings in the picture. Was he not supposed to look? Was there another new rule?

On Friday evenings during the school year, Julian's uncle Maurice—Herzl's brother—came over with his son Peter. This visit would be their first since May. The doorbell rang at eight o'clock. Herzl was resting upstairs in the bedroom. Julian ran down the front hall in his socks, sliding the last few feet. He opened the door and let in his uncle and cousin. Uncle Maurice was divorced, and he was religious. He and Peter wore cro-cheted yarmulkes, which were held in place with bobby pins. Maurice bent down to hug Julian, while Peter leaned back into the shadows near the door. He was twelve, and he had recently experienced a growth spurt. He was covered in a new padding of flesh, and his black hair hung down to his chin. He wore his shirt untucked, had fancy suede sneakers, and carried a leather backpack. He said "What's up?" to Julian. His voice was husky.

Julian took Uncle Maurice's hand and pulled him into the hot, humid kitchen. The window to the garden was steamed over. Rebecca wiped her forehead on her sleeve, then turned to receive Uncle Maurice's hug. Rebecca's hands were coated in lentil loaf batter, and Julian watched them dangle in the air behind his uncle. They were caked in a drying brown crust.

There was a big rectangle cut out of the wall between the kitchen and the living room. Julian could see Peter kneeling on the rug, flipping through Herzl's record collection.

"How is he?" Maurice was asking Rebecca.

"I don't know, something happened this afternoon. He was in the backyard with Julian—" Rebecca began.

Julian walked out of the kitchen and went to kneel next to Peter, who was inspecting a Frank Zappa record he'd taken out of a faded cardboard jacket. Julian remembered Peter prying open a clamshell once on a trip to the beach, forcing it open to

see the live clam. Julian had been content to look at the pretty outsides of shells. Peter liked to open things up and touch them.

Peter handed the record to Julian and said, "Remember when we went with your dad to the radio station?" Julian nodded. Herzl's friend Al was a DJ at WROC. They went the night Al did a phone interview with Frank Zappa, and Peter had gotten to ask a question on the air. As he took the black vinyl disk from Peter, Julian saw his own slender, bony hand, with its thin skin and just a few silky blond hairs—and he saw his cousin's hand, his thick fingers, tough, chewed nails, and two skinned knuckles.

"Do you want to play?" Julian asked his cousin. His voice came out high and flutey, like a faraway child's.

"Where's your dad tonight?" asked Peter.

"Taking a nap," Julian said. "He'll wake up for dinner."

"Let's go up to your room."

The walls of Julian's room were covered in posters from *National Geographic World,* mostly fish and frogs. There was also a souvenir picture from the *Nutcracker Suite* that Julian had meant to take down before his cousin came over. He knew that Peter's walls were painted red and had pictures of Bob Dylan, Albert Einstein, and the kibbutz in Israel that he'd visited. Julian opened the door to his closet, so that it almost completely hid the Sugar Plum Fairy. He leaned against the closet door. Peter locked the door to the room.

"I'm not allowed to lock the door," said Julian.

"Don't you have any privacy around here?" asked Peter.

"Yeah . . ." Julian's voice disappeared. He sighed.

"At my mom's place," said Peter, "there are no walls, just big canvas curtains hanging from the ceiling. It doesn't have rooms, just 'spaces.' I'm having problems with my mom right now." Julian remembered Peter's mom from a long time ago, at a party, holding a cat.

"Do you still have turtles?" Julian asked.

"Yeah. But they're old. They don't move around a lot." Peter suddenly sounded weary, and he flopped down on the floor. Julian flopped down, too. Peter then half-opened his eyes and said, "I brought you something. I don't know. Maybe you wouldn't like it."

Julian tried not to sound eager. "What is it?"

"I found it in the neighbor's recycling," said Peter. "Actually, I found a lot of them."

Julian felt himself clasping his hands together like a beggar. Peter reached into his bag and pulled out a manila envelope, which he tossed to Julian. Julian caught it. He opened the envelope and pulled out a magazine. *Penthouse,* it said. Julian froze. He looked at Peter.

"It's so funny," said Peter. "Look inside. It's really, really funny."

Julian opened the magazine to the first page. On one side was an ad for menthol cigarettes, on the other a table of contents. Julian squinted so everything blurred.

Peter pulled himself across the rug to Julian's side. He giggled and opened the magazine to the middle. It rested on Julian's lap as Peter flipped through the pages.

Julian heard the door to his parents' room open. He heard his father pad into the bathroom, using the cane. Julian's stomach contracted.

"This is the one," Peter was saying.

"My dad is up," said Julian.

"It's okay. The door's locked, remember?" Peter nudged Julian.

Julian was overcome by it suddenly: the thing he'd been trying not to think about all night. It had happened earlier in the day, when he was out in the garden with his father. Right after he closed the little sketch pad, Herzl had pushed against the hammock to stand up. He was up for a second, and he reached his hand out to Julian. Then he toppled over and lay there on

the grass breathing hard. "Get your mother," he said, and as Julian dashed into the kitchen, he wondered if Herzl's hand had been about to squeeze his shoulder apologetically or hit him. Rebecca had helped Herzl up. "You have to go upstairs and lie down," she had said.

"I can't lie down forever," he had said.

Peter nudged Julian again. "Look at this."

Julian looked down at the page. His armpits tingled. He heard the toilet flush, and the door to his parents' room closed with a click. Peter nudged him again. Julian let his eyes focus. It was a picture of two women on the back of a horse, which was standing in a meadow, chewing some grass. It was a beautiful horse, sleek and brown, with a black mane. One of the women was blond and slight, and she wore a white shirt, which was unbuttoned to her waist. A globelike breast pointed toward the sky. She wore nothing on the bottom, and she leaned back against the horse's neck. She had no hair between her legs, like a little girl. The other woman straddled the horse facing her, leaning forward on the horse's back. She held a black riding crop, and her tongue pointed between the first woman's legs.

Julian looked over at his cousin. Peter now had a very serious expression on his face. Julian looked back at the picture. He heard a spatula on a pan downstairs.

Peter said quietly, "I think that one looks a little bit like you."

"Her?" Julian put his finger on the blond one's face. Peter nodded, and pushed Julian's finger away. Julian felt an ache in his thighs. He felt his testicles shift. He heard his mother's footsteps on the hardwood stairs. Rebecca called to them, "Dinner'll be ready in five minutes, kids." There was a pause, and then the footsteps descended. Julian could smell the lentil loaf. He looked at Peter, and Peter was looking at him with a strange, agonized grin. Then Peter stuck out his tongue, making it pointy like the woman in the picture. Julian stuck out his tongue, too, and leaned toward his cousin until their tongues were touching. Julian's penis pushed against his underwear. Pe-

ter put his arm around Julian's shoulder and pulled him close. Julian felt Peter's tongue, large inside his mouth. Julian thought of the Sugar Plum Fairy and moved his own tongue around. Soon they were hugging each other and lying down on the floor. They touched each other's shoulders and arms.

Then it was over. Neither pushed away, they just parted and went back to leaning against the wall. Julian inspected Peter's face. It was red and shiny. Julian still ached between his legs. He glanced down at the crotch of his cousin's pants, but they were very baggy, and Julian couldn't see anything.

"Think about something sad, and it'll go away," said Peter.

Herzl did not come down to dinner.

Rebecca asked Peter about the skateboard he was making. Peter talked about planing down the wood, picking out a finish, and why small wheels were better than the old fat kind. Then Uncle Maurice told them about two-headed tulips that had been found growing next to Three Mile Island. "How can we pray to a God who creates these things?" he said. No one answered.

"Everything in the world is somehow meant to be," Uncle Maurice continued, gesturing around the room with both his hands. "I accept that, or I try to, anyway. But think about it— normally, those bright flowers are the most prized and beautiful part of the plant. Then when you multiply them, they become bizarre—just *wrong*. Who is it that decides these things for us? Is there something we're supposed to learn? If anyone knows, please tell me."

Under the table, Julian's feet moved rhythmically. He was practicing his limp.

After dinner, Uncle Maurice and Cousin Peter went upstairs to visit Herzl. It had been months since Peter had seen his uncle. Maurice had visited after the surgery, but Peter had been in soc-

cer camp. Julian helped his mother fold the tablecloth and make tea. When Maurice came downstairs, Peter was not with him. He explained that Peter was in Julian's room, spending some "alone time."

Julian dashed upstairs. He wanted to tell Peter to take the magazine, that it was too dangerous having it in this house. The door to his room was closed. Julian knocked.

"Who is it?" Peter's voice was muffled.

"Julian."

"Come in," said Peter. Julian pushed the door open. Peter was lying on the bed, on Julian's old Star Trek quilt. When he sat up, there were glossy tear-stripes under his eyes. Julian closed the door behind himself and sat down on the edge of the bed. He was very near to Peter. Peter sniffed and wiped his nose with the back of his hand.

Peter said, "Your dad is sick."

"I know," said Julian. He looked at the Starship *Enterprise,* zooming across his bed.

"I mean, I knew he was sick, but," Peter whispered, "is he going to die?"

Julian looked back up at his cousin and he wanted to beat him. Peter was weeping, and the flesh on his body looked raw and tender. Julian's arms jerked, and for a moment, he felt he would punch Peter in the face, kick him in the belly, push him out the window to fall like a stuffed dummy into the garden.

But then Julian slid off the bed and onto the floor. He pulled his knees to his chest and wrapped his arms around them. He imagined a crisp, sunny autumn day. He imagined walking through a field of milkweed plants. As he walked, the plants started to grow. They grew taller and taller, until they were like trees around him. In his mind, he crawled up a thick stem to a fleshy leaf right below a brown pod. A thousand silk threads encircled him until he was sitting in a bright green capsule. He would hibernate in there, wait until spring. He would not come out until the time was right.

MEMOIR

My father lay in his bed, a white sheet pulled up to his chin. When I entered the attic room where he was living, he turned his head away from the round window and looked at me. His eyes were milking over. I could see his fingers, curling, twisting the bedclothes from underneath. He opened his mouth a little. His teeth were yellow, and they looked huge pushing against his peeling lips.

I sat down in the dark part of the room, holding my green satin purse. I folded my hands across my belly and looked at my father. I started to play with the clasp of my purse, listening to the noise it made opening and closing. Pop. Pop.

"I couldn't get it done," I said. He closed his mouth. "The old doctor's dead." My father turned to face the round window again. I knew he could see the old oak tree with its fresh green leaves, green hands waving in the breeze. The leaves tossed sunshine into the room through the window. The grass of the field was bright and moist, pushing up through the soft black earth. Beyond the field were the hills. Over the hills rose a snaking column of black smoke. Often, there were two columns. Sometimes, when a whole family went at once, there were as many as four or five.

·

So the baby came. The trees turned scarlet and yellow, and leaves piled up like a moat around the house; apples fell to the ground and changed into wine, and drunken field mice dragged them home to their nests. And the baby came. By that time, my father couldn't move at all. He had started to flatten; his hands and feet were desiccated, papery and bloodless, curling backward. Eva from the next house over came to help me deliver. She had two of her own. She'd managed to send one away to the coast, but people there were starting to go, too. She came over to the house ready for a difficult time—she brought armfuls of towels, salves, tonics. But when she arrived, I was sitting up in the kitchen. I was feeling the pains, closer together, pushing at me. I didn't mind them. I liked the feeling. It was a feeling—so I was still alive. Instead of screaming, like Eva told me I'd do, I hummed a song. I couldn't remember where I'd heard it, and only remembered half the words.

Eva closed the screen door behind her when she entered the kitchen. She put her supplies down on the table.

"What are you doing?" she asked me.

I smiled at her. I felt sweat crawl over my cheeks to my neck. I held on to the slatted back of the chair. I never screamed. I never lay down. Eva knelt and cupped her hands, ready when the baby's head pushed through.

•

When I was small, my mother and I used to walk through the field and over the two hills, taking the shortcut to the village. One day, we went to visit Mr. Fryar, the baker. We entered at the front of the shop, as usual. The loop of bells on the door jingled. I went to stand at the picture I liked, while my mother got the bread and soup biscuits. It was a picture of a canyon, where cows waded in a stream, and sheer rock walls rose up. A path was cut in one of the dark gray sides. The valley was crisscrossed by long shadows, but up above the sun shined. A tremendous bird dove, arching away from the sun. I liked to imagine the bird swooping

down among the cows, picking one up in its great beak, and taking it back to a nest of branches for dinner.

My mother chatted with the baker longer than usual this particular day, and I noticed for the first time that there was a little cow looking out from behind one of the grown cow's bellies. Just as I discovered this new detail, I heard my mother call to me. "Come here, dear," she said. "Mr. Fryar is going to show us something very special."

Mr. Fryar, bald and round and all in white, lifted a hinged piece of the wooden counter and let us through. I'd never been in the back of the bakery before. There was a giant mixer with a spade-shaped blade, shelves of tiny bowls, and a long steel table with soft rounds of dough set on it. Mr. Fryar went over to the oven on the far wall, brick, with a chimney and decorative tiles. He opened the oven with one hand, and with the other he pushed in a flat wooden paddle. When he pulled it out, it came with a pan of loaves. He put the pan down on the metal table, and my mother curled her finger to me. "Come and look," she said.

I approached the table slowly, sniffing.

"For the festival on Saturday," said Mr. Fryar, and he held a loaf up with the paddle.

It was a bread baby, shiny with egg yolk. The dough had been shaped into a round little head, ten fingers and toes, and knobby kneecaps. Its torso was a plump braided loaf, with the bread tapering to a twisted cord at its navel.

"Here, take this," said Mr. Fryar. He unwrapped something and handed it to me. "The oven was too hot for the first batch," he said. "They fell apart."

I looked down at my hand. In it was a glossy brown baby fist. The fingers were a little burnt, but the dough on the inside was soft and melted on my tongue. I finished eating it before we got to the end of Mr. Fryar's street.

•

The first person to fall ill was the schoolteacher, Miss Trell. I saw it happen. I was in her class; my seat was in the front of the

room, right across from her desk. I remember the first day, how she licked her lips over and over. Then later that week, I noticed her eyes: that sheen they get, a white greasy layer that spreads outward from the pupil over the iris. The next week, she didn't come to school on Monday. On Tuesday, she had bandages on most of her fingertips. I didn't know her nails had shed, though soon all these signs were familiar in our town. But at the moment, I chose to pay only the slightest attention to the changes in Miss Trell. I'd discovered that every time I glanced at Chess Fulton, two seats over in the next row back, a shudder passed through me. My cheeks crawled, and between my legs there was something sticky. Once, I got excused to go to the girls' room. There I put a finger in the slickness and tasted: salt.

Two weeks after the very first signs, Miss Trell left the school. We were told it was temporary, and we had a man fill in who did tricks with apples and ball bearings. But she never came back, and eventually she was replaced by Mrs. Sargum, who rearranged the seating in the room. Now I was next to Chess. One Friday afternoon, he and I got excused at the same time, and we went to the meeting room with its soft chairs. It was next to the headmaster's office and we had to be very quiet. He unbuttoned my yellow shirt and pulled at the strap of my undershirt. He suckled and I looked at my fingers in his brown hair.

Shortly after that, Chess's mother started showing symptoms. She went into quarantine—at that point it was believed to be contagious—and Chess had to leave school to manage the thread shop.

•

When you're trapped, you want to flee. You try to flee. But a trap—by definition—is something from which you can't escape.

We soon learned that the most unbearable kind of trap is one in which no one has trapped you. In this situation, there is no one to outwit, no one to beseech, and no one to hate.

•

Neither of our village doctors—father and son—knew what to do. The younger one suddenly became religious; the older plied his patients with useless medicines.

A specialist was called in from the city, where he was head of his department at the university hospital. The specialist took a train to the next town over from ours.

He was met at the station by the knife man in his red step truck. The knife man dropped the specialist at the edge of our village, where he was greeted by the sheriff and the older doctor.

The specialist stopped at the inn just long enough to splash some cold water on his face, dot cologne on his wrists, rub some pomade in his hair, and hang up his change of clothing. Then he followed the older doctor to his office, where the specialist set up a makeshift laboratory. After that, they were off again.

They spent the rest of the afternoon visiting the homes of afflicted villagers. When they rang the first doorbell, the specialist smiled to himself—he hadn't made a house call for, he calculated, at least twenty years.

He stopped smiling when he saw the patient.

Late that evening, he looked at the samples he'd taken. The older doctor watched from a chair in the corner as the specialist bent over the microscope. The specialist almost gasped at what he saw—not from horror, exactly, but from admiration (the two aren't as far apart as you think).

This was an organism of great beauty: silky and motile, it danced on the slide, slowing down, speeding up, then whipping around to the point that it just started to break apart . . . and then stopping and resting before it began its dance again.

•

My father let go on Sally's first birthday. I'd moved him to the basement, to try and keep him damp and cool, but by then he had become so dry his arms and legs were ribbons spooled into themselves; his hips had collapsed and widened; the ribs had compressed and begun to crumble. His heart beat slowly—its bulge pushed visibly against his disintegrating ribs.

I've shown pictures of him when he was well to Sally. "That's Grandpa," I say "You look like him. He was the apple grower. Those trees down the road with the sour little fruit—they were once real apple trees, and everyone in the village ate pies from them."

And I show her pictures of her grandmother. "We used to walk over the hills together," I say. "Where the ovens are now—well, there used to be only one oven. And before the sickness came, the oven was in Mr. Fryar's bakery. We had fresh bread every day. You look like your grandmother, too."

Sometimes, Sally asks who she got her tail from. Grandma? Grandpa? She reaches behind herself and holds it; she twists around and studies it. It's a small tail, an extension of her spine. It's lively but dainty, covered in soft brown hair.

Of course people in town wonder about Sally's father. *Who is he? Where is he?* Eva asks. I never tell her.

When my father fell ill and had to stop working on the trees, I got a job at the inn, changing beds and helping serve breakfast. By that time, we rarely had visitors from out of town—just people with special permission to attend funerals. Otherwise, the guests were mostly husbands or wives kept away from their beloveds by quarantine, or spooked people who superstitiously believed that leaving their houses would keep them alive.

I was on duty when the specialist stayed over. I had noticed him come in from the train, with his dark, square-shouldered coat and his cologne and pomade. I had watched him leave again with his kit in one hand and his big book in the other.

It was very late at night, early morning really, when he came back from the old doctor's laboratory. I was at the desk near the door, half asleep, when he woke me up and asked if I had any whiskey.

"Do you want me to bring it to your room?" I asked. He shook his head. I pointed toward the end of the hall, where the lounge was, and told him to wait in there. I got the best

whiskey from the locked pantry, and put the bottle on a tray with some ice and a glass. I walked down the hall to the lounge.

Everybody in town had known that the specialist was coming; everybody hoped he'd have an answer for us; many thought he would save us. But when I saw him sitting in the dim light of the lounge, slouched in an armchair, eyes closed, rubbing his temples, I knew he was nothing, just a man from the city.

I put the tray down on the table next to him. He opened his eyes and thanked me. I sat down a few chairs away. He said I didn't need to stay. I lied and said it was against the rules to leave him alone in the lounge. He took out his deck of cards and started to play solitaire. I watched. I poured him another drink when he finished the first one, and moved to the chair across from him. When he finished that one, I poured him a third and asked him to teach me how to play cards. I already knew how to play most card games. Step by step, he showed me war, hearts, blackjack, gin rummy, and poker. I pretended to be learning them for the first time. He was arrogant in the most gentle way. I let him beat me every time. As we played, and as he drank, he told me about his day. He told me he had played cards on the train, solitaire, and that it hadn't mattered to him if he won or lost. He told me about chuckling to himself before the house call. He told me about what he had seen on the slide.

I poured him a fourth whiskey. Then I reached over, took the cards out of his hand, and pulled him toward me.

•

I've always felt Sally was charmed because of her tail.

I read in a very old book that certain charmed people can read the minds of others. Today, Sally and I sit at the kitchen table. She wears a white nightgown, and I can see her tail flicking underneath it as I bring her a cup of milk. I've told her we're going to play a game, a guessing game.

If she's charmed, then maybe she's safe forever. I want to test her. I want to see how charmed she is.

I take my father's deck of cards from a drawer and shuffle them on the table. Then I pick one out and look at it. The ten of spades.

"Guess which card I have," I say to Sally.

"The six of diamonds," she says and laughs, covering her mouth with her little hand. The nightgown twitches behind her.

I tell her to pick a card and send a picture of it to me with her mind. I try to receive the message and then I say, "The queen of hearts."

"No, it's the seven of clubs," she says and laughs again.

THE SPLINTER

There is a beach on the eastern side of the island. It is a rocky beach, with smooth white pebbles.

It is low tide. A fine foam settles and seeps through the clustered stones. Shells and tangled weeds dry in the heat. The water beyond the beach is huge and blue, and it reflects the cloudless sky. Behind the beach is a grove of short, twisted trees. Their trunks and branches all curve in the same direction, pushed by the constant wind off the sea. Thorns grow between their leaves.

Linda runs down the slope, ducking the lowest branches. Her sandals kick dust and pebbles up in front of her. She carries an empty yellow bucket. She is six.

Last night was very windy, and the terrain has shifted. A root is exposed, the crook of it sticking up. Linda is looking ahead, at the push and pull of the water and the shiny stones. Then, like a cough or a hiccup, she finds herself pitching forward, up and over, onto her head. Her sandal stays caught in the root that tripped her. She comes to rest on her belly, breathing quickly, almost panting. Her legs and feet remain in the shade of the grove, but her torso, head, and arms have crossed into the white sunlight of the beach. She stays like this for a while, at first surprised, then almost luxuriating. Her breath slows back down to normal. She

watches a red mite make its way over the mountain of a tiny pebble. She watches a stiff gray feather shake itself free from an old brown clump of seaweed.

Then Linda starts to feel the pain in her head. She makes herself sit up, folding her sturdy legs beneath her. She lets go of the bucket and puts her fingers to her scalp, pressing on it to find the exact place that hurts. She touches a wet spot. She brings her fingers down and looks at them: there's a little blood, fresh, very thin, orange in the sunlight. She smells it, puts a finger in her mouth and tastes it—a salty, metallic taste. It makes her thirsty. She puts her fingers on the sore spot again. There's a bump there; something from the ground has dug itself into her skin, and a swelling has begun to form around it. The bleeding is stopping already.

She twists to get her sandal from the root. She tugs it free and puts it on her foot, but the tongue of the buckle has broken off. She stands slowly and walks to the wet part of the beach, dragging the foot with the broken sandal. She walks up and down along the water, squatting occasionally to dig for treasure. She finds shells and a sand dollar and the hinged claw of a crab. As she puts these in her bucket, she sometimes feels the bump on her head, presses on it. Usually she comes to the beach in the morning with the kids from next door. Today is just her second time alone. She had hesitated when her father dropped her off, hanging on to his hand, but he'd said it would be okay because it was just for a couple of hours in the afternoon, and besides, he had added, the locals would look out for her.

There is no one else on the beach.

When the sun starts to go down, she walks back through the trees, stopping for a moment at the hooked root, then carefully stepping over it. Then she comes to the other edge of the grove, where the road is, and across the road the tavern where the fishermen drink. A couple of donkeys wait patiently near the tavern, chewing on the clumps of dry grass that grow in the dirt.

Linda feels her sore spot and waits for her father. She hears mu-

sic from the tavern, the whiny instruments and tunes that get faster and faster, played on little records. Once or twice her father has taken her into the tavern for a soda, and the man behind the bar has shown Linda the records, and the plastic disks that go into the middles of them to make the holes fit the record player.

Today she is very thirsty. She would like a soda, brown and smooth, and ice knocking on her teeth. She would like to wash away the tinny taste of blood. But she can't go into the tavern without her father, so she keeps waiting, organizing her objects in the bucket.

He comes before the sun has completely set. He comes down the road with his easel strapped onto his back, and paints and paintbrushes sticking out of his pockets. He's wearing olive-colored army shorts, cut off at the knees, and a T-shirt. His legs and arms are covered with curly yellow hair.

With the bump on her head, and the blood, and the thirst, Linda has forgotten what they talked about last night, and as soon as her father reaches her, she says it without thinking: "I want my mom." He looks angry as he kneels down to her. He takes her shoulders and explains again. Mom is not here. She is in Scotland, which is part of England. Remember? he asks. He repeats what he said last night. Linda will go to Scotland to live with Mom at the end of the summer. Right now, Linda is with him, her father, here, in Greece. He takes her hand and they start up the road. "I'm thirsty," says Linda, twisting away, looking back at the tavern, thinking of a cold soda. Her father tugs on her hand, saying there's plenty to drink back at the house. It's almost dark out now, and the wind off the sea has picked up. Linda walks close to her father, careful not to drag her foot, and brushes against the fur of his arm with her face, smelling oil and turpentine.

They follow the main street, all the way to the top of the village, where their house sits at the end of a skinny cul-de-sac. It is a low white building with a wide door, made of planks and painted blue, that opens onto a small courtyard. An olive tree

grows in the courtyard, and Linda's bicycle with training wheels lies on its side here. In one corner are all the items Linda has gathered from the beach so far, washed with water from a pitcher, and sorted according to texture. Tonight, Linda puts her bucket down in this corner and touches the spot on her head, which is throbbing. When she does it again as she sips the soda he poured over ice for her, her father asks what is wrong. She shakes her foot so the broken sandal falls off. He puts down the onion he has been peeling and comes to her and picks up the sandal. He inspects the broken buckle.

"How did this happen?" he asks.

She says nothing. She touches her head again, pressing on the swollen place. She presses hard. It's an itchy kind of pain, and a little ooze comes off on her fingers. She looks at it. It's not as bloody now, more a clear, sticky substance with blood mixed in.

Her father wipes the onion juice off on his shorts. He feels around on her scalp, and when he finds the bump, Linda says, "Ow!" He tells her to sit still, and he goes to wash his hands. In the sink are the beaks and quills of squid, and on the wooden counter are the squids' flesh and tentacles, sprinkled with garlic and salt. He dries his hands on a piece of cheesecloth and brings a flashlight over to Linda. She watches her father moving around, fast and efficient. She worries about the squid, sitting out like that—she knows they're supposed to be cooked soon after they're cleaned. That way, her father always says, they're tender, more like noodles than rubber.

He shines the light on her scalp, pushes her hair away from the hurt spot. He pokes at it again. "Ow!" Linda says again.

"It's one of those damn thorns," he says. "How did you get a thorn in your head? Did you bump into a tree?"

"I fell," Linda says. "I broke my sandal."

"You fell on your head?"

She nods.

"Wasn't there anyone else at the beach?" he asks.

She shakes her head, looking at her sandal, which is balanced

sideways on the floor. He covers the squid with an upside-down bowl, then disappears into the bathroom. He comes out with a pair of tweezers. He takes a pack of matches out of his back pocket and lights one, burning the angled metal pincers. He prods the splinter a little bit. Linda's body stiffens, and she grabs on to his shorts. He tries to get the points around the thorn, but he has trouble finding a place to grasp. He spreads the skin around the thorn, pressing down. Linda squeezes his leg through the soft green cloth. He curses. "I love you, Daddy," Linda says, crying. She feels the tears creeping from her eyes, and she tastes the salty mucus that flows from her nostrils and rounds the curves of her lips. She sniffles and reaches up to wipe her face.

"Just hold still," says her father. He digs with one point of the tweezers, and her scalp starts to bleed again.

He announces that he can't get the thorn out. He pats her on the shoulder and pries her fingers from his leg, then goes back to the bathroom. This time he comes back with a bottle of rubbing alcohol and some cotton balls. He dabs her scalp with alcohol and tries to push her hair back into place.

He fries up the squid quickly, leaving out the onion. They sit at the low table near the windows. The house is divided into three rooms: there is this room, with the kitchen in one corner; Linda's father's room, which is big and has a view of the village's roofs and the sea beyond them; and then there is Linda's tiny room, which holds just her cot and the chair where he sits and reads to her at night.

The throbbing calms down, and Linda does not touch the spot on her head. It's late in the evening, the hour when he would normally be telling her to get ready for bed, when she would be picking out a book or asking him to tell her "Chicken Little." But tonight, he's forgotten about her bedtime. He paces back and forth in the main room, a glass of wine in his hand, cursing himself and asking her questions.

"I knew I couldn't do it," he says. "I told her. I told her. This was exactly what I was talking about. I said I wouldn't know

what to do if you got sick. Why did she have to do this to me?"

"I'm not sick, Daddy," says Linda. He does not hear her.

"She said to take you to Marisu if something happened. Marisu! Of course this would happen the one time she goes to Athens." Marisu is the next-door neighbor they get yogurt from. "I told your mother to take you with her, to take you to Edinburgh now. Right? Remember?" Linda nods. But she doesn't remember. She remembers her parents staying up and talking and talking before Mom left, and when Mom said, "I'll see you soon," Linda thought she meant tomorrow. But that was a long time ago, or at least it feels like it was.

Her father paces. "I can't do it. I can't do it," he says. He punches the kitchen counter.

"Time for bed," Linda finally says in the same tone of voice he usually uses.

He looks at the white plastic clock over the stove. He stands still for a second, then turns the flashlight on again and shines it on the swollen part of her scalp, where the blunt end of the thorn is pillowed by a blister of skin and fluid. He drips more rubbing alcohol onto it. "Okay, Linda, I don't want to try anything else—go get ready for bed. I'll be in in a minute." But then he follows her into the bathroom. Linda sees him in the mirror, watching her as she stands on the stool to brush her teeth. He looks like he's trying to smile, but his forehead is wrinkly and his eyebrows are pulled together. Linda steps off the stool, then climbs up onto the toilet to pee, then undresses herself, kicking off her shorts and underpants. She leaves her clothes in a pile on the bathroom floor and says to her father, who stands near the door, "Carry me like a baby." She's never done this with him before. It's a bedtime game she has with her mother. He picks her up, with one arm supporting her neck and the other under her bent knees, and he tilts her body toward his chest. She says, "Ga ga goo goo, me a baby." He carries her to her bed, smoothing her hair over the growing lump.

He puts her down on her cot, pulls up the sheet and cotton

blanket, and puts his hand on her forehead. He asks how she is feeling.

"I'm *not sick,* Daddy," she says. She touches her fingers to her sore spot. He reads to her, and she falls asleep quickly. He almost wakes her up to make sure she's all right, but he stops himself.

He remembers the boat ride from Athens to the island, about six weeks ago. Most of their bags were in the cargo deck below, but Nora, Linda's mother, carried the girl's plastic tote bag. It had several zippered pockets and a picture of a dancing elephant on it; inside were Linda's sneakers, a change of underpants, and a couple of her favorite books. In their hotel room in Athens, Nora had also thrown in Dr. Spock's *Baby and Child Care*—"In case she gets seasick, Tom."

"That's a good idea," he said, meaning it, but it sounded cruel and sarcastic. Nora rolled her eyes back and pushed air through her nose. It seemed too complicated to him to go back through the exchange and apologize.

They went to different decks on the boat. Nora watched Linda run up and down the upper deck, laughing at the gulls who picked at their feet with their beaks. He went to the bar. He had his easel with him, and he leaned it against a pole. He ordered a glass of ouzo and smoked a brown Turkish cigarette. There was a French businessman who was going to one of the islands to discuss building a television station. Tom practiced his French with this man. They joked about Americans. Tom was always ready to ridicule the kind of people he saw wandering supermarket aisles like zombies. Then he started to feel sick. They were further out on the water, and the boat was rocking. The easel slid down and hit the floor with a clatter.

Tom excused himself and went up to find Nora and Linda, dragging the easel behind him. Nora had wrapped her white Spanish shawl around herself. She looked up at him and laughed. He tried to grin. Linda ran over and looked up at him.

She asked her mother what was wrong with Daddy. He made his way as quickly as he could to the stern and vomited into the sea. When he came back, he sat on the chair next to Nora's, and Linda came over and patted him on the shoulder. Nora took Dr. Spock out of the bag and read aloud. "Why didn't we bring any arrowroot biscuits!" she said, laughing. He laughed too. He was feeling better. Linda climbed up the side of the chair onto his lap, and Nora got him a bottle of club soda.

They had laughed together, he remembers now. Every time they laughed together, he thought it would be okay. He thought that everything they had said and done to each other could be remedied. He believed the things they talked about in the dark, late nights meant nothing as long as they could laugh the way they did when they first met. For Tom, once the sun rose, it was almost as if those conversations hadn't actually happened: they became distant and abstract, as fleeting as dreams. But even in the daylight—over breakfast, with the *Herald Tribune* spread out in front of her, or at a museum, standing before a Miró etching— Nora acknowledged those nighttime subjects: betrayal, disappointment, regret. And she still laughed with him.

When they arrived on the island, they discovered they had left Dr. Spock under one of the canvas chairs on the boat.

Now Tom gets up and plans tomorrow. He starts pacing again. He takes a couple more glasses of wine and tries to read. Finally, though, he sits back down in his chair by Linda's bed, and falls asleep there.

When Linda wakes up the next morning, her head is throbbing again. Her skin itches around the thorn, and she runs her nails over it. She gets out of bed and walks, naked, into the kitchen. Her father is stirring a spoonful of instant coffee into some hot water. It's bright in the main room, but he still shines the flashlight on her head, parting her dark hair to look at the splinter. He says it doesn't look good. He asks her if she's been touching

it a lot. She shakes her head and takes a piece of bread off his plate. He cuts another slice of bread, spreads butter and marmalade on it, and passes it to Linda.

"We're going to see Marisu's grandmother today." This was Tom's inspiration at six this morning, when he woke up and started pacing again.

Linda remembers the old woman who lives all the way on the other side of town.

While she slept, her father made a new tongue for her buckle out of a paper clip. He helps her into her shorts and T-shirt and sandals.

They walk down the hill into the village. Linda skips ahead of her father, then runs back to meet him. "No more skipping today," he says.

"Why?" she says.

"Because of your head."

Marisu's grandmother is very happy to see them. She speaks only Greek, so everything is communicated with sign language. She pushes them down onto chairs in her sunny whitewashed parlor. She wears a long black skirt and a black shirt and shawl, and her head is wrapped in black cheesecloth. She brings in bowls of canned fruit cocktail for each of them. Linda devours hers, sticking the spoon all the way into her mouth, swinging her legs as she chews. The old woman fusses over the girl, stroking her cheeks. She takes out pictures of her great-grandchildren, not the ones from next door that Linda knows, but ones who live in Thessaly. Linda nods. She's not very interested in the pictures but knows she's expected to be polite. After a while, Tom takes the woman's wrist and pulls it toward Linda's head. He parts the hair for her and shows her the swelling. He shows the woman his worried expression and shrugs. He says, "Can you help me?" hoping she'll understand something from his voice. The old woman pushes the skin down and tries to squeeze the thorn out. Linda screams, and Marisu's grandmother keeps pushing and forcing, talking to the girl in Greek. Linda continues to wail, and finally

Tom can't take the violence of it anymore. He pulls the woman's hands off his daughter's head. He puts a sheepish, apologetic expression on his face for her. She gets a pencil and a piece of brown paper and writes something in Greek.

Tom takes Linda away as fast as he can, trying to act respectful, but angry at the old woman for hurting her. What had he expected Marisu's grandmother to do? He wanted her to be wise and sympathetic, to transcend language, and to have an ancient herbal remedy that would make the blister go down and the splinter come out. Linda is still crying and clutching his hand as they walk back up the hill. "I hate her! I hate her!" she is saying.

"It was wrong of her to squeeze so hard," her father says.

"Not her!" says Linda. "I hate Mommy."

There is a young woman at the money-changing window of the bank who speaks some English. Tom greets her and asks her to translate what's written on the slip of paper. He picks up Linda and rests her on the ledge that is meant for pocketbooks. The young woman wears a short denim skirt and panty hose, and a single comb encrusted with rhinestones holds back the hair over her right ear. Most of her hair falls in her face as she reads the note. For a second, Tom feels a familiar receding, and his eyes blur as he notices, as if looking at a landscape from a great distance, the zigzagging pattern that the young woman's hair makes against her skin, which is the same color—though a much paler tone—as the piece of paper she holds. He imagines mixing the color of the notepaper on his palette, then adding white to get the skin. And then he hates himself. He closes his eyes and presses his thumb and forefinger against his lids, then makes himself tune in to the young woman's voice. She says that the note directs him to take the little girl to Mr. Gregos. She looks at Linda and smiles. Tom becomes conscious of the shiny stripes left by his daughter's tears on her cheeks.

"Who is Mr. Gregos?" he asks.

"Oh, he is very good," says the young woman. She gives

Linda a chocolate wrapped in pink foil. She draws a map of the streets and puts a circle where Mr. Gregos is.

"Is he a doctor?"

The young woman laughs and shrugs, looking like she does not understand. She tosses her hair back and waves at Linda as they leave. A picture of the Dr. Spock book in the shade of a canvas deck chair enters Tom's mind.

He carries Linda now. She's tired from all the walking they have done. He lets her hold the map and pretends she is helping to navigate.

Mr. Gregos's place is another low, whitewashed building, but with a tiny dome on top. The door has a brass plaque bearing what Tom guesses is his name in Greek, then, written on a piece of loose-leaf paper, the name in Roman characters. It's spelled differently than by the woman at the bank. Here it's Gregous.

Her father puts Linda down and knocks on the door. Linda touches her head. It's still sore from the old lady. Forgetting everything for a moment, Linda turns, expecting to see her mother, but then reminds herself: Mom is in Scotland, which is part of England. Linda looks toward her feet and sees a shell sticking out of the ground. She squats down and tugs it out. There is a clear indentation in the dry, hard-packed earth. She shows the shell to her father. "How did it get all the way up here?" she asks. He says he doesn't know and knocks on the door again.

The door opens now. Linda stands, staring, with her mouth open. Her father steps back and puts his hands on her shoulders. In the doorway is a dwarf, only a few inches taller than the child. He has long arms, and his hands dangle past his bowed knees. He has a trim white beard and white hair. He wears a dark suit and a shirt buttoned all the way to his neck, but no tie. He does not smile but nods and says something in German.

"Not German. American. English," Linda's father says. Linda has backed up into her father completely.

"English," the dwarf echoes. He steps aside for Linda and her father. Linda's eyes are level with the dwarf's mouth, and she sees

that his front teeth, both bottom and top, are gold. She looks at his feet. He wears black shoes, one of which has a built-up sole several inches thick. Linda has a windup dump truck that is missing a wheel, and the dwarf's feet make her think of it.

Neither Linda nor her father moves. What would Nora do, Tom wonders. Nora's not timid. She would probably enter Mr. Gregos's house. If he were crazy or evil, wouldn't the woman at the bank have given him a clue? Tom gives Linda a gentle tap on her back, and tells her it's okay. She looks up at him, squinting. He understands she's probably skeptical. They enter the house, and the dwarf leads them down a short, dim hallway, and through a door into an office.

It's just an office. There is a big oak desk and a leather blotter. A green desk lamp and piles of papers and journals in Greek and German sit on the desk. On the wall is a matted reproduction of a Monet water lily painting. There are also two diplomas or certificates, very official looking, in Greek. Across from the desk are two matching chairs with chrome frames and woolly orange seats. Mr. Gregos climbs onto a raised chair behind his desk, and he motions for Linda and her father to sit down.

Linda approaches one of the chairs and touches its arm, but then turns and waits to be lifted onto her father's lap. For a second, Tom feels embarrassed, feels she's acting like a baby; then he remembers that she could be crying from fear, or she could be laughing at the dwarf, and he pulls her up onto his knee. Behind the desk, with the squat bottom half of his body hidden, Mr. Gregos looks intelligent and authoritative. Linda's father smiles, starts to relax. Mr. Gregos smiles and shows his gold teeth. Linda smiles for a second, but then turns and presses her face into her father's shirt. The three remain like this for minutes, Mr. Gregos observing the father and child, and Tom trying to smile, wanting Mr. Gregos's approval.

Finally, the dwarf gets down from his chair and comes over to Linda. He puts one of his big hands on the back of her head. Her father points to the place where the thorn is lodged. Mr.

Gregos nods. He does not touch it but points to the floor and says something in German. Suddenly uneasy again, Tom lowers Linda off his lap. Mr. Gregos puts his hand out for Linda to hold, leads her out of the office, across the hallway. Tom follows as they enter another room. This one is small, windowless, all white like a doctor's office.

The dwarf's hand is dry and warm, and squeezes Linda's hand firmly as he leads her. He smells good, clean, not perfumed. He wears a ring on his pinkie, which presses into Linda's pinkie. The metal is smooth—it does not hurt her. She looks around this room. All the shelves and cabinets are low, as if they were built for her, like ones in a playhouse or a nursery school.

Mr. Gregos gestures for Linda's father to wait behind her, near the door, and he takes a key ring out of his jacket pocket. He opens a cabinet and pulls from it a plastic tray full of small pharmaceutical bottles and tubes. He picks up a tube, uncaps it, punctures the seal with the reverse end of the cap, and squeezes some clear jelly onto his fingers. He takes Linda's hand again, then dabs the substance onto her puffy scalp. Linda's father steps forward. Mr. Gregos puts out his hand to stop him and taps Linda's scalp. She does not flinch. Tom understands: it was just an anesthetic. He smiles, nods. This is fine. He knows what he's doing, this dwarf.

Then Mr. Gregos reaches into the cabinet again. Linda's father watches him, and it seems to be all in one motion that the dwarf produces a bottle of spirits, uncaps it, tips it back over his mouth, and swigs from it. Then he pulls Linda's head toward him and puts his mouth over the bump on her scalp. Tom jumps forward, but the dwarf has already done it. Linda doesn't feel the pain, just a jagged tugging, a drawing out. The dwarf looks up at her father and smiles, showing him the intact thorn held between his gold teeth.

Tom's heart is racing. He wants to strangle the dwarf, or pound him into the floor, splitting him in two like Rumpelstiltskin. But he just kneels down and turns Linda to face him.

"Are you okay?" he asks his daughter.

"I'm fine," she says. "Is that it?" she asks, twisting away from her father to point at Mr. Gregos's mouth. Her father says yes, it is. "Thank you," she says to the dwarf. He nods and takes the thorn from between his teeth. He pulls a handkerchief from his pocket, wraps the thorn in it, and hands the bundle to Linda. Tom stares. The dwarf rummages in the tray and finds another tube. He hands it to Tom. Then he writes his price down on a notepad, elegant European numerals. Tom has just enough money along. Tom nods, says *danke,* the only German word he knows, and hurries Linda out of the house.

As soon as they round the corner, Tom stops, pulls Linda aside. He looks at her head. It's greasy with ointment, but the swelling has begun to go down. Linda gives him the handkerchief package to keep in his pocket, then holds up her hand for him to take. It's the same hand the dwarf held. Tom suddenly does not want to touch Linda. She waits, looking up at his face, her brown eyes looking into his. He makes himself wrap his hand around hers. It is soft, and a little sticky. Her bones are tiny. He could break them with one forceful squeeze.

They walk up the hill toward the house. Linda's father starts to think about his paintings. He remembers how it used to be, to spill color onto the canvas. It felt like it came from his body, some organ with no name. Ever since he arrived on the island, he's been painting perfect landscapes, blue skies, rippled water, sunsets over the whitewashed village. He hates them now, this afternoon. *What's wrong with beauty?* he has been saying to himself all summer. But they weren't beautiful, just flawless.

Linda looks down at the dust clouds that she kicks up with each step.

UPSTREAM

In early August the family went on vacation to Seattle. Late in August, back in Hadley, Massachusetts, David was dropped off after his softball team lost badly to East Hampton. When he walked into the living room, he saw that one of his father's students, Emily, seemed to have fallen down on the rug and his father seemed to have fallen on top of her. David was frozen in the doorway, wondering if Emily was laughing or crying, and if the two of them needed help, when his father noticed him and croaked, "Go away—I'm sorry," looking almost at David, but not quite.

David stared for one more second—just long enough to notice that Emily's skirt was pushed up around her hips, and that his father's belt was unbuckled. Then David turned and dashed upstairs to his room. He locked the door behind him and sat on the edge of his bed. His head pounded. Tiny gray squiggles, like the silverfish in the basement bathroom, danced in a space in front of him that he'd never noticed before; it was as if his eyes were made of glass, and he could suddenly see the surface of the glass instead of looking through it. He rubbed his eyes, but when he opened them, there were more squiggles. He was panting. He felt that he should try to scream, but when he opened his mouth, he made

a low, creaking noise, an embarrassing noise that made him blush, even all alone in his room. He flopped backward, bouncing a little on the mattress.

He lay there with his feet dangling. He stared at the ceiling, at the cracks in the plaster he'd been staring at almost his whole life. And for the first time in many years, he thought of how he'd seen the shapes of monsters in the cracks when he was little. There they were: a hulking, gorillalike shape, a fishy, fanged shape with one leg, and a four-armed phantom with a pointy hood floating into a corner of the molding.

A little while later, there was a knock at the door. David said nothing. He just lay there. He heard his father's voice. "David? David, I want to talk to you"— and David was about to get up and open the door when his father finished his sentence— "before Mom gets home." David pulled his feet up onto the bed and curled on his side. He slept until his mother knocked on the door and told him to come downstairs for dinner. At the table, David didn't look at his father.

So it was less of a surprise to David than to his older sister Michelle when, parked in the lot of the Rite Aid one evening in the first weekend of September, Labor Day weekend, their father and mother twisted around in their seats and looked back at the children and announced that they would be separating. For how long, they did not know, but they hoped it was not forever, for they both loved each other very much still. They said they didn't want to fail like so many of their friends, other couples who had met in college and married and stayed in the area, and whose marriages collapsed. David watched his father's mouth as he spoke—and he understood why his father had a reputation for being a great teacher. He was so eloquent; he spoke so easily and sincerely.

When his father started the car, David said, "I have one question."

"Yes, sweetie?" his mother said.

"We'll still have Christmas together, right?"

His father reached his hand across the bucket seats and squeezed David's mother's thigh. "Of course," his mother said, and she placed her hand on top of his father's.

The next week, school started, and David got his first sixth-grade homework assignment: "Write about something important that happened over summer vacation."

On Saturday, David's mother's friend Sally came over with her Volkswagen Vanagon, and David's father and mother and Sally moved his mother's belongings, some furniture, dishes, and silverware out of the house. David's mother looked thinner than usual to him, smaller in her sneakers and old blue jeans. His father made jokes. Sally gave David a hug. Later, right before they drove away, David was coming down the stairs when he heard Sally ask his father, "Why is he here today?"

David heard his father clear his throat. "We thought about having him spend the day with a friend, but then it seemed like that would be worse, to come back, you know, and have everything different," his father said. "Michelle decided not to stick around."

Later, David sat down to write his report. He could barely wedge his legs in under his low white desk where a year ago he'd had to sit on a cushion to work. He held a brand-new pencil with a fresh pink eraser, but for the first time in all his many years of writing reports, he couldn't think of what to say. He had writer's block. He looked at the college-ruled loose-leaf sheet in front of him with the assignment written on the top line: "Write about something important that happened over summer vacation."

He couldn't begin. It was as if he had lost the ability to think clearly. Images of the summer bombarded his brain; he tried to think, to pick one out of the mess, but they were a blurry, shifting jumble. He remembered his mother with watery eyes and a pile of tissues telling him she had allergies. He remembered

Michelle showing him a jar of nail polish that she claimed to have shoplifted. He remembered arguing with Jason about whether the Red Sox sucked; he remembered gluing glitter on a birthday card for his grandmother; he remembered his father storming out of the house and slamming the door after his mother won a game of Scrabble, and his mother laughing until she cried. But none of this was worthy of a report.

He closed his eyes. He breathed in and out, like his mother did when she needed to calm down, to "focus," as she said. He'd seen her this way in front of the potter's wheel, hands coated in slip, resting on a bowl that had started to go lopsided, breathing in slowly, then out even more slowly.

Finally, he began. "In August my family went to Seattle," he wrote. He hadn't wanted to be obvious, to write about the family trip the way everyone else would. But he had no choice. He was desperate. He described the Space Needle, an island where they visited an authentic pioneer house, and then the locks:

The locks are where the water level changes, and they move the boats up and down. In Seattle, it's where the river meets Puget Sound. Next to the locks are the Salmon Steps. They have built steps for the Salmon who are swimming upstream to go back to spawn in the place where they were born, they live in both salt and fresh water. You can go underground to a room. The room is dark, but a whole wall of it is made out of glass, the glass gives you a view of the salmon. The current is very strong, you can see it pushing, making bubbles and white foam. But the Salmon are strong too, and they are very big. You would see a salmon pushing and pushing against the current, it looked like it was going nowhere then suddenly it would jump up to the next step.

He'd stood down there for half an hour, while his parents and Michelle got fried clams and sodas up on the cement pier. The sunlight had poured through the churning water on the

other side of the glass, beams slicing into the turbulence and illuminating the spotted silver scales of the tremendous fishes. They were so sleek and muscular, the salmon, and so determined, their winglike fins and fanned, striated tails beating, gills opening and closing, revealing momentarily the slits of bloody redness underneath.

Finally, his mother came down to get him, and she stood there for a minute with him, watching, and squeezed him close to her, saying it was chilly.

When David read over his report, the only thing he didn't like was "very big." It didn't capture what he was trying to describe. He went over to his bookshelf and pulled out the thesaurus that his father had given him as a fifth-grade graduation present. *Sizable, great, large* . . . all boring words. He sighed and looked up at the cracks in the ceiling. Then he erased "very big" and wrote "monstrous."

He got a good grade, an A minus. The teacher had made check marks in the margin next to the parts she liked best. "Watch for run-on sentences and review rules about capitalization," she wrote at the bottom of the page.

Early in October, David started to think about his Halloween costume. He talked it over with his mother one night when he was staying over in her new house, an A-frame in the woods that she was renting from her pottery teacher. David told his mother he wanted to be scary, *really* scary—not some lame prefab Freddy Krueger hands, or Jason hockey mask, or Scream ghoul costume. He wanted to be a monster, ferocious and powerful.

David's mother got the supplies, and when he stayed with her again the next week, they made a papier-mâché head. They kept a book with pictures of the Creature from the Black Lagoon open in front of them on the table. They gave the head bulging eyes on either side, and a flat nose, and a gaping mouth

full of tiny, pointy teeth. The next day, when it had dried, they painted it green and black, with dark red lips.

On Halloween, Michelle went to a party dressed as a belly dancer. She wore a bikini top covered in sequins, and she had gotten her belly button pierced for the occasion. As she was leaving the house with her friend, she'd whispered to David: "I shaved down there." David's cheeks got hot. "Does Mom know?" he'd asked, but Michelle had just winked at him and put her finger to her lips.

David's father drove him around trick-or-treating.

"Arrrrrrrgggggghhh," David would growl when people opened their doors. He wanted them to have heart attacks, or run out into the road waving their arms for help, or at least wet their pants. They did none of these things at the places he visited. Some people would say, "Oooh. You're scary," or "Eek."

The last stop of the night was a big stone farmhouse, a place where groups of college kids had been living since the time when David's parents were students. When the door opened, David smelled pot smoke and heard loud music with a mechanical, popping drumbeat and a moaning female voice. They pulled him into the living room, two boys and three girls, and gave him cookies and a sip of beer through a straw and then had him stand with his arms outstretched saying "Argghh" to get into character while one of them pointed the Polaroid. A boy wearing antennae on his head asked David what planet he was from, and David said, "Earth." "What did you say?" the boy shouted at him, and David shouted back, "Earth!" They took an extra picture, and one of the girls walked him out to the car.

"That took a long time," said David's father as the window slid open. He was listening to jazz on the car radio in the dark.

The girl leaned into the car to hand the snapshot to him.

"Oh! Professor Berg," the girl said. David's father looked at her. David could tell his father didn't recognize her. "I'm Julie Doyle, Emily's friend."

"Oh yes," said his father, "Julie. How are you."

"I got a letter from Emily. The fellowship is working out for her in Paris. Have you heard from her?"

"No," said his father, sighing and looking at the road. "Actually, it was a surprise that she left so abruptly."

"Well, you know. Shit happens. Everything changes," said Julie Doyle.

"Yes, I suppose so," said his father. Julie continued to stand there, leaning into the car. Then she dug in her pocket and got out a stubby pencil.

"Do you have a piece of paper?" she asked. David's father looked around in the car until he found a long Stop & Shop receipt. "Here's my number," said Julie, "in case you want Emily's address or something."

"Thank you," he said, tucking the receipt into his jacket pocket.

"Your son's so cute," said Julie. "Definitely the best costume we've seen here all night."

"I thought he was out of his monster phase two years ago," said David's father. "Time to start meeting girls."

"My mom made my costume," David said from inside the papier-mâché head. His breath made a warm, damp environment in there.

"What? Can't hear you," said Julie, pointing at her ear. "Well, nice seeing you, Professor Berg. Call me if you want."

The week after Halloween, David got assigned another report. This one could be about anything, as long as it used five words from the sixth-grade vocabulary workbook. On Friday night, he sat down on the rug in front of his mother's woodstove and wrote:

There have always been and will always be monsters. Monsters are terrifying, usually they are very big, but even the smallest ones scare people. They are *independent,* needing

nobody to take care of them. They are at their *apex* when they are roaming around the land, causing mayhem. That always happens at night, especially when the full moon is an *orb*. They are at their *nadir* during the day, when they are alone in their cave waiting for it to get dark. Most monsters are very *wily,* but some are not very smart, they are just strong and frightening.

Late in November, right after Thanksgiving (which David and Michelle spent with their mother and Grandpa Fergusun and Grandma Winnie in Deerfield), David walked up the driveway, holding a note from his homeroom teacher. He didn't open the sealed envelope, but he knew the gist of what was inside. It would tell his father that although he'd done some promising work early in the term, his grades had been slipping, and it would single out the C-plus vocabulary report. It would say he seemed to have trouble concentrating, that he was slow getting from one class to the next. It might mention that he'd been caught cutting class twice, reading monster comics with a seventh grader, Skylar, in the boys' room. His father was out when he walked into the house, so David dropped the envelope on the kitchen counter and hurried up to his room, closing the door. He waited until he heard his father's car on the driveway, and then he braced himself for the questioning. But when David looked out the window, he saw his father get out of the car with Julie Doyle, who was helping him research an article and had been coming over now and then.

David opened his door and sat quietly on top of the steps, his heart pounding so hard it hurt, at first willing his father not to find the note; then, as he heard sounds of the kettle being filled, papers being shuffled, crackers pouring out onto a plate, and Julie laughing, David began to will his father to find the note.

David found himself moving down the steps one by one on his rear end, a slow-motion version of how he used to slide down them as a little kid. From the very bottom step, he could peek into the kitchen. He saw the envelope, glowing white with the mid-

dle school's seal stamped on it, and he saw his father standing next to Julie, his right hand in her long brown hair, fingers combing through it, then grabbing and pulling. Julie slapped his hand playfully, and David's father said, "Look, we're not trying to prove he was a saint, just that he wasn't a total anti-Semite."

"But I've read his books, Berg. I'm not dumb. Remember I was in your class?" Julie said. "You don't remember."

David's father said, "Look, we're talking about a writer's *persona,* don't you know. Just because he's writing in the first person from the point of view of a character very similar to himself, it doesn't mean that person *is* him."

Julie groaned. "That's not what I'm saying."

On the steps, David coughed a quiet cough, then waited to see if either of them noticed.

"He removed all the good and reasonable parts, and created a character based on the darkest part of himself, the part he hated the most. If you read the letters he wrote to his friends and his editor, you see that he was a kind, rational guy. *And* deeply disturbed by the nationalistic turn that was happening in politics," David's father said, raising his voice slightly.

"He beat his wife!" said Julie, also raising her voice.

Then his father grabbed Julie's wrist and pulled her close. "Maybe she liked it," he said. Julie laughed, shaking her head.

David crept back upstairs and crawled into his room. He was suddenly aware of the drafts; the icy November air seeped into the room as if the wall was perforated with thousands of microscopic holes. He kicked off his shoes and got under his comforter, pulling it up over his chin. He stared at the fish beast on the ceiling; he imagined it half-hopping, half-swimming, chasing the phantom further and further into the little black space where the molding met the plaster. When he was little, he'd made up a sound for each monster. The fish beast had a gurgling, hiccupy noise. David remembered that his mother had laughed when he first demonstrated it, and he had crossed his arms and sulked, saying, "It's not funny, it's *scary.*"

• • •

The day before Christmas vacation started, David sat with his parents—*between* his parents—in the office of the school counselor, Mr. Daniel. It was their second meeting with him. Mr. Jolly, the school principal, had recommended that the family see Mr. Daniel once a week. In the principal's office a few weeks earlier, Mr. Jolly had said that, while the school believed in giving individual attention to students, the bottom line was that David's grades needed to improve or he would be held back. He'd also mentioned that he found it worrying that David's parents had taken ten days to respond to the note from Ms. Lanegan.

"No one sent me that note!" David's mother had said, her open, upturned hands batting the air. His father had looked down at his knees.

Now Mr. Daniel smiled at David and then at his father and his mother. The week before, he'd mentioned that he had friends who were friends of David's parents. His ex-wife had taken David's father's class at Smith, "Precursors of the Postmodern." David liked Mr. Daniel. He seemed to be able to get David's parents to sit quietly and talk gently to each other, something that hadn't happened much since his mother had moved out, despite what they'd said in the Rite Aid parking lot. Mr. Daniel had made them renew their promise to spend Christmas together. And this time, Mr. Daniel had brought something for David: a comic book that had been his own when he was a kid, a monster comic book, with pictures of bloblike beasts carrying women into a swamp.

"Thanks!" David said, thumbing through the pages.

"I don't think it's healthy, this monster obsession," said his father.

"All little boys like monsters," said his mother. She looked over at Mr. Daniel.

"I mean, at his age . . . ," said his father.

"Why do you like monsters?" Mr. Daniel addressed David.

David looked at the counselor, who, with his pale, freckled face and rumpled oxford shirt, looked like a kid himself. David shrugged. "I don't know. They're strong and powerful. People have to do what they want or the people get killed. Plus they don't have to talk all the time—monsters don't have to explain themselves."

"Do you have to explain yourself?" asked Mr. Daniel.

"Yeah, I'm doing it right now, aren't I," said David, smiling at the young man to let him know he wasn't being a brat to make Mr. Daniel's life hard.

On December twenty-fourth David's mother brought an overnight bag to the house, and after an awkward first hour, it became the kind of Christmas Eve the family always had: his parents made a big batch of eggnog, and his mother laughed when his father, pretending to slip, dumped extra whiskey into it. They had a goose stuffed with chestnuts, and beans covered in butter, and creamed spinach. They all sat in the living room after dinner, holding their stomachs and saying they were going to throw up. Then David's mother opened a bottle of red wine, and she and his father drank the whole thing. David and Michelle went to bed early, right after a second bottle had been opened. They knew their parents needed time to wrap presents.

In the middle of the night, David was pulled out of a dream as he became aware of noises coming from underneath his room. He turned over on his side and hung his head off the bed, staring at the floorboards, listening. Slowly, he recognized what he was hearing: his mother's little moans, rising in volume, his father's heavy breaths, which started to turn into grunts.

David slid out of bed and tiptoed out of his room and into the hall. Michelle was there, too. She was waiting for him. David and Michelle looked at each other in the blue near-darkness. Moonlight glinted off Michelle's new eyebrow pierc-

ing. They smiled at each other. Michelle reached out and squeezed David's shoulder.

David felt that a strange episode in his life had ended, as easily as his dream had floated away. When he got back into bed, he looked up at the ceiling, and even in the dark, he knew the cracks just looked like cracks.

But in the morning, everything was wrong. David recognized his father's strained, false smile, and his mother's shrill imitation of cheer. After waffles and presents, his mother left abruptly without saying good-bye to his father; she slammed the door of her Rabbit and backed down the driveway fast.

Starting the new term at school, David pretended to try harder. He'd put a look of concentration on his face in class. He'd write reports with long, complicated sentences using three-syllable words from books in his father's library. But he had no idea what he was doing. He felt as if he had forgotten how to read and write. When teachers talked, they sounded like they were underwater—David couldn't distinguish their voices from all the other noises, the footsteps in the hall, doors opening and slamming shut, birds outside the classroom windows, cars starting in the parking lot, lawn mowers, the gym teacher's distant whistle, and the breathing in and out of all his thirty classmates who knew something that he didn't.

In history class, they were studying ancient Greece. They looked at maps that resembled irregular quilts where places with crazy-sounding names were represented by colored patches, and the teacher talked about things that had happened thousands of years ago. David stared out the window, rubbing his eyes, or doodled with his erasable ballpoint pen. On the day they made yogurt ancient Greek style, David found himself claiming to be allergic to dairy, and he spent the class collating and stapling mimeos instead. Before they moved on to Rome, the teacher gave the class an assignment to write a report on

the voyage of Odysseus over midwinter break, which was really just a long weekend, a Friday and a Monday off.

David's father had a couple of days free from teaching, and announced to David over breakfast on Friday that he'd decided it was finally time to paint the upstairs bathroom and hallway. Wouldn't David like to help? he asked. It would be fun.

"No thank you," David said, looking into his bowl of granola.

"How about you, kid?" David's father asked Michelle, who was already zipping up her parka near the door. Michelle just rolled her eyes.

When they were done eating, David's father dragged the big ladder up from the basement. David watched him while he put a drop cloth down on the floor in David and Michelle's bathroom.

David went into his room and lay on his bed. He intended to do well on this history report. He was the smart kid—he thought—didn't anyone remember that? He'd show them all how precocious and clever he was. After hours of doing other things (he organized his comic books; he called his mother), he sat down at his desk and opened his heavy textbook to the page the teacher had marked:

"The Voyage of Odysseus."

David tried to read, but couldn't concentrate. He couldn't get involved in the story. He started flipping the pages, ignoring the words, glancing at the pictures. But then he saw something that made him stop: an illustration of a creature standing on a small island in the middle of a frothy sea. This creature was built like a man with no neck, it was wearing a tattered fur poncho, and in the middle of its forehead was a huge, raging, bloodshot eye.

David spent the long weekend reading as much as he could about Cyclops—he found his father's copy of the *Odyssey,* he scanned several encyclopedia articles, he looked at a coffee-table book of paintings by Redon. But by Monday night, the last few hours of his break, he still hadn't written anything. His floor

was covered in books and pieces of paper, but he still felt that he had nothing to say, nothing he wanted to share with his history teacher anyway.

His father had finished painting the hallway that morning but had left the ladder there. Now he was out to dinner. Michelle was in her room, listening to music. David opened his door and tugged on the ladder. It was lighter than he'd expected. He pulled some more, and it slid toward him on the drop cloth. He went to Michelle's room and knocked. When she came to the door, he asked her for help, and together they moved the ladder into his bedroom.

"Why do you want it in here?" Michelle asked. "Daddy can change the lightbulb."

"I don't know," said David. "It was in the way out there."

After Michelle left, he took one of his favorite pens, a permanent black Sharpie, from his desk drawer. He dragged the ladder across his floor and climbed to the top step. And in the middle of the forehead of the hulking neckless ceiling monster, he drew a big, black, wide-open eye.

At their meeting the next week, Mr. Daniel said he'd been thinking about monsters. "We've talked about how they're strong," he said, "and how they don't have to answer to anybody, right?"

David shrugged.

David's father said, "Let's get off the subject of monsters. *Please.*"

But Mr. Daniel continued, addressing David: "But also, they're kind of like babies, aren't they," he said. "When they're happy they laugh and pound their chests. When they're mad they roar and cry and rip things apart. They don't hold back, do they? Whatever they're feeling, they just let it rip. Right?"

David laughed. "Yeah," he said. "They're just like, *Roar!* I'm hungry. *Roar!* I have to pee."

Mr. Daniel laughed too, and said, *"Roar!* I'm mad. *Roar!* I'm sad."

David laughed again. Then Mr. Daniel said, "David, if you don't mind, I'd like to have a word alone with your folks."

Later that day, David learned that when Mr. Daniel was alone with his parents, he'd suggested that the family think about private school. Over the next few weeks, David and his mother and father visited five schools. Together, they filled out applications for four of them, sitting around the kitchen table at David's father's house one night. David noticed the formal tone in his mother's voice when she spoke to his father, as if they were now just business partners who had started out as friends long ago.

The Quaker school asked for an essay, and David submitted the report he wrote about going to Seattle. He made the grammatical corrections his teacher had suggested and reread it sitting in front of his father's computer. "All in all," the report had concluded, "the best thing about my whole trip to Seattle was the salmon." He now added, inspired for the first time in months, "I have never seen such majestic beauty in any other animal. Swimming upstream takes superhuman strength. Most people would give up before they even got anywhere. But the salmon have to go home. It's their nature."

In early May, David was accepted to the Quaker school, and spring finally came for real. The breeze was warm instead of chilly, the mud from April's rains dried up, the apple trees were budding. David was counting the days until the end of the semester. He did a minimum amount of work, ignored the other kids. He was even cool toward Jason, his oldest friend. Every day after school he would run through the front door of the house, drop his bag in the kitchen, and run back outside through the

rear door, over the long stretch of lawn and the scrubby field to the small river that flowed along one border of the property. There, he would sit and inhale the sweetness of the leaves overhead and the pungent, almost chocolaty smell of the mushrooms that had sprouted on the banks in the shade of the oaks and maples. There wasn't much life in the river yet—a few small fish, spiders, and one old turtle that David thought he recognized from the summer before.

One day, as David walked back to the house, damp and a little chilly from the riverbank, he saw that Julie Doyle was dragging a huge, olive-colored army duffel bag up the steps to the door. David's father carried a smaller bag, which looked heavy. David guessed it was full of books.

"Hey, guy," said Julie to David. She smiled at him. Her lips were smooth and pink. Her teeth were crooked.

"Hey," said his father, breathing hard, mussing David's hair with his free hand. "Julie's going to rent the spare room for the summer."

David shrugged. He had the urge to ask his father why he bothered lying, but he kept his mouth shut. As David expected, the spare room became a storage space for Julie's things, but she slept in his father's room every night.

On the last Friday of his career as a public school student, David visited Mr. Daniel's office.

Mr. Daniel had a whole big stack of comic books for David. When he handed them to David, David's stomach turned over and his throat contracted. He started to cry. It hurt, his tear ducts opening and his sinuses contracting, and the tears themselves were very salty, stinging his skin as they crawled down his cheeks.

"I'm such a loser," he muttered.

"No, you're not," said Mr. Daniel, and he gave David some tissues.

"Well, anyway, thank you for the comic books," said David, turning away.

"It's my pleasure to pass them on to you," said Mr. Daniel, opening the door for David.

David made sure to walk out of the big concrete school building slowly, so he wouldn't forget how it felt.

That summer, David spent every afternoon until dinnertime down on the riverbank, watching the water get more and more full of plant and animal life.

One day in July, he was squatting on a rock, sucking at the sweet raw center of a piece of grass, when he noticed something in the water. It was white and oblong, and though the water flowed rapidly downstream, the thing was staying in one place. David watched it, trying to make it out under the ripples. Suddenly, he noticed an eye, and something flapping behind the eye, almost a gill, David thought, but ragged and chunky. There was a mouth up front, opening and closing, slowly gulping, and where a tail would be on a fish, there was a stub, with a tiny shard of fanlike, translucent skin beating side to side. There was one scaly, silver patch near the head, but the rest of the flesh was spongy-looking and loose. As he watched, a piece of the gray flesh peeled back and broke off and was carried rapidly away from the creature. David found himself panting. This was a true, real-life monster, a terrible pathetic thing, a dying thing, a thing already dead but living at the same time.

David ran up to the house and into his father's study, where his father sat reading. He grabbed his father's arm and pulled him outside and through the grass to the water. It was still there, the thing, but it had changed even while David had been gone. More flesh had come off, and there was a bit of spine exposed.

"How bizarre," said his father.

"What is it?" asked David, his voice cracking.

"It's a salmon," said his father. "But it must be pretty old. Atlantic salmon don't usually get so banged up. You'd think it would have died a long time ago, huh?"

"That's not a salmon," said David, his throat closing.

"Sure it is," said his father. "I remember from when I was a kid. You know that river near Grandpa's in Vermont? After they've been swimming upstream for months, they don't look very pretty, they sort of fall apart like this."

"That's *not* a salmon," said David again.

"It's part of natural selection. A lot of them don't even make it home."

"They don't?" said David. He lowered himself to his knees on the brown dirt of the riverbank.

David could feel his father's eyes on him. They were silent for a while; then David felt his father's hand on his head, messing up his hair.

"David," said his father.

David said nothing. He kept watching the beast through the rush of water. He was breathing hard; he felt his inhalations, deep almost to the point of pain, and his exhalations, rapid expulsions of hot, moist vapor. David was still a boy. He only came up to his father's collar. He wanted to crush his father, to pulverize him, to make him into nothing. But he knew that if he sprang up and beat at his father with his fists, his father would be puzzled and disappointed, but unhurt. So David remained there, crouching, while his father patted him on the head. A minute later, his father turned and started walking back up the hill.

The thing had been moving backward inch by inch. It was just a matter of time, David knew, before the water overpowered it.

"Good-bye," David whispered to the fish, when he was sure his father was out of earshot. "Good-bye."

THE RIVER AND UNA

The search party called from a mechanic's shop. They were at our house ten minutes later. I ran out to the pickup as soon as it pulled into the drive. My mother stood on the edge of the porch and held on to the wooden railing with one hand; with the other, she shaded her eyes. The man in the driver's seat rolled down his window and reached his hand out for me to shake, which I did. He was the assistant baker from Minton's Bread Shop in town. I'd never seen him out of his white hat before. I didn't know the man in the passenger seat, didn't recognize his lean face and mustache. His arm was around a blanket-wrapped bundle: my sister.

I went to the other side of the truck and opened the door. The mustached man carefully slid out of his seat, then lifted my sister out after him. She was small in his arms; he was very tall. He held my sister like a bride, under her knees and head. Her bare white feet dangled from the blanket. I reached out and touched an icy pinkie toe.

"Come inside," I said, staring at my sister's feet another moment, then turning toward the house. I looked over my shoulder every couple of steps to make sure he was coming. The plains stretched out flat on either side of our house. The gravel drive divided two squares of shorn lawn, then there were

taller, paler grasses, then fields of wild wheat, then brambles.

The man followed right behind me, up the porch steps. My mother said to him: "Can you carry her into the parlor? My back is bad." She opened the screen door, and he tilted my sister a little so neither her feet nor her head banged against the door-jamb. My mother showed him the big wicker chair next to the woodstove. He bent his knees and lowered my sister into the chair, onto its flowered cushions. As he did this, the blanket fell away from her head. Her black hair was damp and clung together in bunches, and a few tiny twigs and stones were twisted in the locks. The man rested his cheek on her forehead for a moment before he let go of her.

I went over to her and looked at her face. It was covered in scratches. One cheek was swollen and bruised; there was a small bruise under her mouth. Her eyes were closed. I knelt down and listened.

She was breathing.

"Una's wild," said my mother. "If she doesn't change . . ." It was the beginning of a threat or a warning.

"It's not her fault," I said, as always—but this time I couldn't meet my mother's eyes as I said it.

The man had backed up to the front door.

"Do I owe you anything?" my mother asked. He stared at her for a moment, as if he hadn't understood. Then he shook his head slowly, and finally turned to leave. In a minute, I heard the pickup starting up, and the gravel crunching as they backed away.

My mother and I looked at each other. She stood with her arms folded low, her bony hands cradling her elbows. The blue veins stood out beneath her thin white skin—one zigzagged across her forehead, disappearing at her hairline into her brown and gray hair; another ran an uneven path from below one of her ears and across her throat.

My mother covered her face with her hands for a moment, then brought them down, sighing. She said she was going upstairs to the bathroom to get gauze and liniment.

Usually, I looked forward to being alone with my sister, to hearing about her brave or naughty adventures. But that morning, I wasn't sure I wanted to know. I put my mouth close to her ear. "Una," I whispered, "who were you with this time?"

My sister opened one eye and looked at me. A corner of her mouth curled: almost a smile. The tip of her tongue came out and licked the center point of her top lip. I looked into her open, unfocused eye. The surface looked greasy. I shuddered. Then I leaned away a bit and whispered the question again: "Come on," I said, "who were you with?"

The eye closed. When I realized that she wasn't going to answer me, I said, "You can tell me later." I went into the kitchen, put the tin kettle on the range, and rinsed out the teapot. For the thousandth time, I went over the morning of Una's disappearance in my head, but it blended into other mornings in my memory. I couldn't bring back the details. There had been so many mornings, so many quarrels, so many times Una had threatened to leave. As I spooned tea leaves into the pot, I asked myself—why had she finally gone through with it that morning, after that quarrel?

All of a sudden, there was a thump and a crash. I ran back into the parlor, then stopped short. The chair was empty and over-turned, and the blanket lay in a heap halfway between the chair and the front door. I hurried down the hall and out onto the porch. Una was running, naked, bent over at the waist, hands in two tight fists. She ran away from the house on the gravel.

I sprinted after her, down the drive. I could hear my sister panting before I got close enough to catch her. I finally got to her just before she reached the road. I grabbed her from behind, one arm around her belly, the other around her ribs. Her breasts were round and heavy and cold; my skinny forearm and my knobby, little girl wrist were buried under their weight as I pulled her back to the house. Una let me drag her, but she didn't help.

My mother was standing in the parlor when we got back in. She held the kettle up as I entered, pulling my sister with me.

My mother looked away from us as she showed me the bottom of the teapot.

"Now what are we going to do?" she said.

The bottom was charred, black, and a hole had burned all the way through.

The feeling of Una's cold body stayed with me for the rest of the day. Even after my mother had handed me a flannel robe to wrap my sister in, I couldn't forget the weight of her breasts on my arm, and the ghost of her belly's cool mass continued to envelop my fingers. Though we had always shared a room, for years I had been careful to turn away as she dressed or changed into her nightgown. And I never undressed in front of her—at night, I raced upstairs to slip into my pajamas; in the morning, I waited until she had left the bedroom before I put on my school clothes. Una always laughed at my modesty: after all, my figure was all angles and straight lines, and on my chest sat two hard little nubs, as if pieces of my ribs had sprouted and grown outward. I knew that when I was a very little girl I had run around on the hot days of summer completely bare. But I also remembered that when my mother told me I couldn't do that anymore, I had been content in the frilly sundresses she slipped over my head.

While I watched over Una in the parlor that afternoon, and tried to shake the feeling of her flesh from my skin, my mind kept wandering back to one afternoon when I was twelve and Una was fourteen. For one week each summer, we used to rent a cottage on the man-made lake near the river's head. And long after she should have, Una rejected her swimsuit because she liked the feeling of the sun-warmed water on her skin. We used to go on rowboat rides—one of us would row out, then pass the oars to the other for the ride back. This time, when I had rowed out to the middle of the lake, I fell asleep on the way back, lulled by the rhythmic sound of the squeaky oarlocks and the wooden oars scraping the wooden boat. When I opened my

eyes, we were floating near the little beach our family shared with the other renters in the cluster of cheap bungalows. Una had peeled off her shorts and bandanna-patterned top, and lay back against the bow wearing just her sandals. Her fingers, thick, with chewed-down nails, stroked the black, glossy tendrils that grew on the mound between her belly and her thighs. The faintest scent wafted over to my side of the boat, something that reminded me of the slick newborn kittens I had seen in the Loomises' barn once. I covered my nose with my hand, and breathed in the artificial coconut of suntan lotion, but still I watched her, my eyes locked to the motion of her hand.

When we finally drifted to shore, our mother was standing there with a big yellow beach towel, which she threw over Una as soon as my sister stepped out of the boat.

"Young lady," she said quietly, glancing for a second behind herself at the bungalows, "this has got to change."

Una never changed, though, she just intensified, and although she wasn't beautiful like the fashion models and movie stars we saw in magazines, every man who saw her watched her, every man who came close to her breathed harder, as if she were a vapor that he could inhale.

When our father left us suddenly, permanently, we found a note on the kitchen table telling us not to worry about him—"I'll be fine," the note said. "If there's one thing that every town needs, it's a piano teacher." He had taken all of his sheet music with him, and his metronome.

Our mother blamed his leaving on Una. "It's you," she said to Una. "What man could live under the same roof? He did it to protect all of us."

The doctor came the day after Una was found. He examined her in the parlor. He told us she was all right; she just needed a lot of bed rest.

My mother sent for Joe Loomis, the oldest boy from the

house across the road. He was strong—sometimes I'd go to a school wrestling match and watch him compete. He helped us move my sister to the bedroom upstairs. My mother offered him a little money, but he said, "That's all right, ma'am." I thought he smiled at me as he drank his tea in our kitchen.

I stayed home from school for a couple of days, but then my mother said I had to go back.

It was late autumn. After school, I'd take the shortcut home. I'd run upstairs to see my sister, and sit with her until dinnertime.

The cuts on her face healed, and the bruises turned green, then yellow, and then they faded away. After a week, the doctor visited to check on her. I sat on my bed across the room, and watched him touch her wrists and forehead, and tap her knees and chest.

"She's a lucky girl," the doctor said, "all the damage was superficial—look how she's improving. More rest. That's my only prescription."

When he left, I lay down on my sister's bed next to her. Her eyes were closed; she seemed to have fallen asleep. Her hair, famous in Lime Mills for being so long and wild and black, was clean and brushed now, fanned out on the blue flannel pillow. My own hair was short, like a boy's, and cowlicked in a single brown curl over my forehead. I studied the shape of my sister's body under the quilt. For the first time in many years, I didn't feel shy looking at her. Her chest was broad, and those big, soft breasts spread across it. Her hips curved above her round thighs. I touched my own chest, felt its flatness and the two dense, tiny bumps. I put my hand on my sister's cheek and turned her face toward mine. Her brows were thick and velvety; they almost met in the middle. With my thumb and forefinger, I touched her eyelids, and slowly pushed them up to look into her eyes.

Her eyes were dull and unfocused. I shuddered, but kept looking.

She had changed now, I knew, the river had changed her for good.

I let go of her lids. She licked her lips, which had been dry and peeling since she'd come back from the river. I thought of all the older boys at school who'd kissed those lips in empty classrooms, in cars, in the woods. I felt my own lips with my tongue—thin and slack, they had never touched a boy.

"Una," I said, "how did it happen? You can tell me—you know I don't care. Tell me. How did you fall into the river?"

She licked her lips again.

"Did someone push you? Did you slip? Was it cold? It was very cold, wasn't it?"

She moved her mouth, stretching it around the whispered words: "I was pulled."

One day, about two months after he helped with Una, Joe Loomis was waiting outside my classroom at the end of school.

"I have to do an errand for my mother in town," he said. "Would you like to come with me?"

I nodded casually while I buckled my book bag, as if invitations like this were an everyday occurrence.

We went down to Division Street, where everyone could see us walking together, and we stopped in at the notions shop. He bought a yard of pink satin ribbon and a whole bolt of muslin.

Then Joe walked me home. He walked me right up the gravel to the front door. He said, "See you later." Then I watched him cross the road to his house, carrying the bolt of cream-colored fabric. He lived with his two brothers and two sisters, his father and mother, and Grandma Loomis. Behind the big old Loomis house were the hills that curved around and sloped into town. I imagined living there, how it would be warm and smell like food. I imagined looking out the back windows on a rich, rounded view instead of the flatness on our side of the road.

When I got inside, I ran through the house and tore upstairs to the bedroom. I pushed the door open and dropped my book bag

on the floor. "I went with Joe to buy notions!" I said to my sister.
She licked her lips.

The doctor kept visiting once a week. But he had stopped
telling us Una was well. I'd watch him shake his head as he
backed out of our bedroom. He'd go downstairs and close the
door to the parlor, where he'd confer with my mother.

One night I lay on my bed smelling my hands. Joe Loomis had
bought me a turnover at Minton's after school, and I could still
smell the butter and apples. I had been waiting all day to tell my
sister how Joe had unwrapped my turnover for me, how steam
had risen in the cold autumn air. I looked over at Una. Her hands
were moving under the quilt. I watched them for a minute. Maybe
this little action was a sign, I thought, a sign she was getting better after all. I went over to her bed, turned on her lamp, and pulled
back the covers. Her white sleeves were edged in lace. Her nightdress was pulled up around her waist, and her legs flopped open,
muscles slack from the months in bed. And her fingers worked in-
dustriously. Where the hair had been so thick and dark and glossy,
it was now dry and gray, and she pulled the shriveled strands out
one by one, leaving the flesh looking plucked and bare. I grabbed
her hands and pulled the nightdress down, but when I saw her doing it again a few minutes later, I just turned away.

That year, winter was hard and sudden. I pushed Una's bed
closer to the window so she could watch the snow fall.

It was the coldest season the valley had seen in years. For the
first time I could remember, the river froze. Joe and I walked
down there one afternoon. We took the back path through the
woods to the riverbank, and we sat down on a fallen maple. I
leaned up against the tree's base; the twisted roots were frozen
and exposed. I had on Una's old coat. It was soft white wool,
with fur as black as Una's hair circling the collar and lining the

hood. I'd outgrown my own coat and had taken this one from
the cedar closet one morning. I'd stood on the stool near the
front door and inspected myself in the mirror. If I pouted a little, I even looked a bit like Una. My mother made no comment
as I left the house in it every day, and I always took it off before
entering the room where Una lay.

Sitting close to the frosty ground, I was shivering, and Joe put
his arm around me. I moved closer to him, and we looked down at
the surface of the ice. It was thick but transparent; it had frozen
quickly. Beneath the ice, we saw brown plants and rocks that glit-
tered with mica. Down the river a little bit, a man stood on the ice.
He held a short rod and was digging in a bucket. A string hung from
the rod, and he hooked something from the bucket onto it.

"Can fish live in this cold?" I asked Joe Loomis.

"It's not the cold that kills them, it's the suffocation if the ice
gets too thick," said Joe. "But that doesn't really happen in
rivers—ponds and lakes maybe, but not rivers."

The man dropped his line into a hole we couldn't see. He
stood very still.

I pulled the hood around my head so that my face was framed
by the black fur. It was soft and it pressed against my cheek. It still
smelled like my sister's perfume: roses and spice. I watched Joe.
He was looking at me with half-closed eyes, and a smile I'd never
seen before. He slipped his hand, in its soft suede glove, inside the
hood. I felt it between the back of my neck and the fur. He pulled
me toward him and tilted his head. Then he kissed me. His lips
were cold and stiff, but inside his mouth, it was hot and slippery.

When we parted, we looked back at the man. He was pulling
something up from the water. It looked like an eel, long and silver, flopping on the ice. The man took a wide stick from his
bucket, and he slammed it down on the wriggling thing's head.
Redness spread out from the fish and disappeared on the ice.

I pressed myself into Joe's jacket.

* * *

When I got home, I planned to go straight up to the bedroom. I couldn't wait to tell my sister that I'd finally been kissed—*by Joe Loomis, on the riverbank!* But as I hurried down the hall toward the staircase, I glanced into the kitchen and saw my mother. She had been spending more and more time with her hands covering her face; that afternoon, she was sitting at the table, the points of her elbows balanced on the Formica, her palms supporting her chin, her fingertips pressing against her eyelids. There was something on the table in front of her. I walked slowly and quietly into the kitchen and stole a look at the object: it was a tarnished brass frame, with shiny glass. When I got closer, I saw that, behind the glass, there was a photograph of my father. I hadn't seen this one before, or I didn't remember it. In it, he was very young, with a mustache, and he sat in front of a piano. His long fingers rested on the keys, but he was looking straight at the camera, grinning.

I bumped the toe of my shoe against a table leg, and my mother brought her hands down and looked at me. We looked at each other.

"Someone needs to find him," she said. "Find him and tell him."

I nodded. Then I turned and left the kitchen. I didn't run up the stairs, I walked; I didn't want to go into the bedroom. I wanted to leave the house, to run across the street to Joe. I pushed open the bedroom door.

Una's head was turned toward the window. I looked at her hands resting on top of the quilt. They were as wrinkled as an old woman's.

She had been running a fever for the past three weeks, and the doctor had stopped attempting to cure her. "All I can do is try to make her more comfortable," he had said to my mother the last time he visited. Una had changed a little every day, so minutely I sometimes forgot she was changing. But then I also forgot how she used to be.

Her lips had lost their color. Her teeth pressed against them.

I heard something from my sister's bed. A scratching sound as her lips moved against each other. As I went over to her, I realized that I still had on her coat.

"What are you saying, Una? What do you need?" I put my ear close to her face.

I looked at her eyes but could hardly see into them, so buried were they in the dry, loose folds of her lids.

"I wish they had never found me," she said. "They should have let me be."

"Don't be silly," I said, stroking her forehead, even though a wave of revulsion went through me. I started to sweat, and I pulled her coat off, letting it fall to the floor.

"I was gone, already gone," she said. "I'm already gone."

"You'll get better," I said, like I had been saying all along. I was a liar. And I was thinking of Joe.

There was silence.

I turned to look out the window at the flat, snow-covered fields. I wondered what Joe and I would do next. Would he put his hand under my shirt? Would he put his lips on my neck and leave a mottled red mark for everyone to see? What would I do if he wanted to go further? Would he ask me to marry him, I thought, and then I imagined myself in a glorious white dress, holding a bouquet of primroses.

Then, all at once, I remembered every detail of the morning that Una had run away. We were having breakfast, our mother and Una and I, in the kitchen before school. It was still dark out; the faintest purple glow was starting to come through the windows. Una's messy hair was in her face, and she wore a blouse that our mother had tried time and again to hide in the pillowcase full of clothes for the charity shop, but that Una always pulled back out. It was tight, too tight: her flesh pushed at the seams, the buttons were pulled taut against their thread. Our mother pressed her thin, creased lips together and shook her head. "Una," she said, and my sister turned her head away, pretending to watch something out the window. My mother went on: "Una,

you're going to be eighteen next month. You'll be done with
school in the spring. What are you going to do? This can't go on."

"What can't go on?" I said. A jay alighted on the windowsill
and pecked at a wormlike streak of dirt. Una laughed at it.

My mother addressed me: "A girl can't live like this forever, like
Una lives." Then she reached across the table and put her hand
around Una's wrist. Una finally turned and looked at our mother,
the corners of her mouth curled spitefully. "When I was eighteen," our mother said, "I got married. I married your father. I
managed his schedule and kept the books. I billed his students
and organized recitals. I had you, Una. What will you do?"

"I don't know," Una said, using the disdainful tone of voice
that she reserved for my mother, "but hopefully not *that*. I
mean, Daddy didn't exactly stick around, did he? I heard he's
living in the city with a girlfriend."

"Damn you," said our mother, who never cursed. She
slammed her free hand down on the table—not a punch but a
slap, which made a hollow, belching sound. I giggled nervously.
My mother ignored me and said to my sister: "You are never
going to grow up. You are never going to grow up." She was still
holding on to Una's wrist. "You are never going to grow up."

My mother kept repeating that sentence, and slowly, Una's
smile changed, and her eyes opened wide. Una was staring—
not at our mother anymore but at a spot in space, over the center of the table, where she seemed to be watching a terrible
scene play itself out. She started to breathe harder, then to pant.
She stood up and pulled her wrist out of my mother's grasp.
She tore away from the table, running out the front door. I
stood up to go after her, but my mother told me to stay, to let
her get it out of her system. She was missing for a week.

Now I turned back to her and stroked the dry, tangled hair at her
temple. "Una," I said, "did you know that fish live under the ice?"

North Curve

My mother was ironing. I was sitting at the kitchen table with a stack of index cards, studying for my vocabulary test. On the plain side of each card, I had written a word; on the lined side was the word's definition that I had copied from the blackboard. *Sycophant, lugubrious,* I read, *epigraph, epitaph.* I tried not to peek.

The radio was tuned to the classical music station. It was the one thing my mother would listen to. For over twenty minutes, the only sounds in the room had been the hiss of the iron and a single bow, moving across a cello's strings. My mother had taken violin lessons as a child. Whenever she talked about those lessons, she said that they were the happiest hours of her life. I didn't like the sound of the cello, but I didn't hate it. And it was better than silence. Or talking.

When the doorbell rang, my mother and I looked at each other. I've always thought, *That's when my heart started to hurt: when the doorbell rang.* But who knows how it really was. Anyway, I remember that I sat still. My mother sighed and shook her head as she walked past me.

It was a courier from the sugar factory. A boy, with a white cotton cap in his hand. He was panting. His eyes were wet and they jumped around the room; for a second, he looked at me. Then he hung his head.

This is what the courier had come to tell us: that my father

had been shot. He'd been shot by a thief. The thief had been wait-ing under a dock while my father helped load some containers onto a barge. My father had been shot in the neck. He was dead.

I ran to the bathroom and vomited. When I came back out, my mother was giving the boy a dollar. He put his cap on and disappeared from the doorway. I heard him stumble a couple of times as he ran down the stairs. Then my mother shut the door.

I squeezed her arm as she went back to the ironing board. She pulled away from me and picked up the brown shirt she'd been working on. "I guess I'm done ironing for the day," she said. Then she giggled a high, harsh giggle that I had never heard before.

The police never did anything. My father's friends from work were vague and told conflicting stories. We never saw his body. A couple of people said that the thief had pushed my father off the pier and into the water after shooting him. And even though the factory had surveillance cameras trained on both of the piers, management claimed that the videotape had been blank when they tried to play it back.

Years later, I found out that my father hadn't been shot, he'd been stabbed. And he wasn't at the factory when it happened, he'd been here in the North Curve. He'd been at the Belle Claire, in fact, just a few doors down from where I work now. The Belle Claire has been around forever. Unlike the other places around here, it's a house, not an apartment, and it has dusty red rugs and chandeliers missing half their teardrop-shaped jewels.

When I was first looking for a job, I walked into the Belle Claire. I don't know if I really wanted to work there, or if I just wanted to see where my father had died. It was morning when I pushed open the door. The beaded curtain rapped against the glass pane. Evelyn herself came down the curved staircase to greet me. Her skin was thin and creased, and she had deep tri-angular grooves under her cheekbones.

I told her I was in need of employment. That's how I phrased

it. I was wearing a white blouse and a pink skirt. I said I was new in town, that I was from the countryside, that I was saving up to go to stenography school. I knew better than to tell her I was a dropout, that I'd been working on my own for three years, meeting businessmen in bars and hotel lobbies. I knew better than to tell her that I had stopped only because I'd pretty much exhausted the downtown market, and I'd started to feel like I might get in trouble. I knew better than to tell Evelyn that I'd had more things—human things and thing things—inside me than I could count or remember.

She took me to a back room, which smelled like roses and mint liqueur, and had me unbutton my blouse and show her my breasts. She felt the weight of them in her white, bony hands. Then she hired me. I never showed up, though. After I left the Belle Claire, I went downtown and ran into a girl I knew, a barmaid from one of the hotels who was an escort on the side. She told me that Barry Snee was expanding his business. I lucked into this job: I was the last to be hired. The pay is better than anywhere else. The sheets are clean. There are three bathrooms. And the bedrooms here are modern, done in chrome, vinyl, and brand-new paneling.

One night, I had to stay overnight at work because I'd misplaced the keys to my apartment. So I was here when Barry arrived early in the morning. He was sitting at the front desk in his overcoat, waiting for the coffee to brew, scanning an accounting ledger, when the buzzer sounded.

Barry looked over the top of the ledger at me.

"Maybe it's just a delivery," I said.

Barry laughed. "You wish."

I unclipped my hair and stuck the *Daily Mirror* under the couch.

It wasn't a delivery. It was a man in the brown uniform of a sugar factory foreman. He stood in the doorway with an orange hard hat in his hands.

"Her," he said to Barry, pointing at me.

"Well, good," said Barry. "She's the only one here right now."

I stood up and took the man's hand. He was a large man, soft-bodied, and his hand was like a slab of steak—a fillet—cool and damp.

We went to the best room, the one in the corner. I looked out the window while he undressed. To my left, I could see the whole North Curve: three drawbridges, a tugboat, the closed-down box warehouse, and the canal itself, shimmering green like antifreeze. In the distance straight ahead, I saw the gold-leaf dome of Borough Hall, and the rooftops of a few of the taller downtown buildings, places where I had made money in hotel rooms, boardrooms, bathrooms. To my right was the slope, where the streets became wider and grander as they went uphill, finally ending at the park's edge with mansions and plane trees too far away for me to see. When I was a very little girl, I would close my eyes and listen to my mother's classical music on the radio and imagine marrying a man who lived near the park. He'd buy me a piano and a reclining arm-chair.

"It looks like it's going to be another rainy one," I said, turning around to the sugar factory man. He sat on the edge of the bed in his briefs, which almost disappeared in the meat of his thighs and his drooping belly.

"It's been a real rainy season," he said.

"It's good for the canal, though." I said it like my father used to. "Good for business, a nice high canal."

"You're right," he said, "good for business, but bad for the piers. The piers are wood. Wood rots."

"Yup," I said.

"What's that?" he asked. He raised one of those big hands and gestured at my shoulder.

"Nothing," I said, "a flower. It's been there a long time. I got it done when I was drunk."

"I can see the flower," he said, "but something's underneath."

• • •

One month to the day after my father died, my mother had been standing at the ironing board. The iron was hot, but she didn't have anything left to press. For the first time, she wept. She wept and pressed the iron against the flesh of my shoulder. I had just taken a bath, and my skin was still damp. I heard the sizzle of steam as she leaned into me. The feeling had been chill for a second, then hot, hot.

When I walked into the tattoo parlor five years later, I wasn't drunk: I was stone sober. I pulled up my sleeve and showed the scar to the proprietress, a squat woman with long whiskers drooping from either side of her upper lip.

"Cover this," I said.

The woman looked at the scar for a full minute. "It's shaped like an arrow, pointing at your heart. It's a mark of love." She reached up from her stool and ran her finger along the ridges. "I don't want to cover it."

I rotated my arm and considered the old burn. It had been so long since I had seen my mother. I had left soon after the incident with the iron—though not because of it; I'd left because of a yellow-haired boy who had his own place near the city's one beach. Standing in the tattoo parlor, I imagined my mother the way she was when I walked out carrying my borrowed duffel bag: in my mind, she was still sitting by the window, listening to the radio. The thought of it made me dizzy. I swore to myself that I would go and visit her that very day . . . but even as I made the promise, I knew I would break it, as I had broken every promise I could remember making.

Then I pulled my money from my pocket and pointed randomly at a picture of a lily from a row of ink-on-paper samples.

In the bedroom with the man, I just repeated, "It's nothing," adding, "don't worry."

He folded his arms in front of him and slouched, looking at the floor.

I breathed in and out. I looked at the skin hanging above his elbows. I took a few steps toward the bed and sat down on the rug. Then I picked up one of his feet, with its crumpled toes and fallen arch, and started to stroke it. He didn't move. He pulled his arms closer to his body. He was shivering.

"I'm sick," he said.

"I can make you feel better," I said.

"No," he said, then. "*No,*" kicking at me with his foot. I fell backward, but I wasn't hurt. I stood up and moved away from the bed, back over to the window. Behind the curtain was a buzzer in case things ever got out of hand. I could reach it from where I stood.

"If you're sick," I said, "maybe you should—"

"I can't go home," he said.

He pulled on his socks first, then his stiff, creased pants and the shirt with epaulets and four pockets.

From an early age, I knew that my father sometimes visited the North Curve. One day, on my way back from elementary school, I saw him through the green windows of the B71 bus. He was wobbling down the sidewalk, his arm around the shoulder of another man in brown, a guy from the factory that I'd met once or twice. My father hung on his friend. His knees buckled with every step. Both men were shaking, holding their bellies from laughter, I'd thought. But now it occurred to me: he may have been weeping, my father.

I walked across the room to the man sitting on the bed. His seams strained as he bent over to tie his shoes. I put one hand on each of his shoulders and pressed my lips against his forehead. He was burning hot.

"I can't go home," he said again.

PERSONAL FOUNDATIONS OF SELF-FORMING THROUGH AUTO-IDENTIFICATION WITH OTHERNESS

Prologue.

Recently I came across a journal entry from my adolescence. I am living a lie, it said. How truly, truly sad.

Chapter One. Beginnings.

I never fit in with my family, kind as they were. As a youth, I never really found friends. Acquaintances, perhaps, but no one I could consider my soul mate. I had a dark imagination; I came to a nihilistic outlook too early to express my thoughts properly. Or perhaps I should say an existential outlook, for although I was painfully aware of mortality, I did not reject the idea of truth altogether. I felt that there was a truth for myself that I dared not examine—the stakes of self-examination felt much too high for me at that age. So I crawled about with a black haze around me, speaking as little as possible, refusing to participate in any of the social customs that seemed to me then a desperately thin patina of etiquette in the face of our inevitably animal natures. While my sister made friends and started to attract males, scampering about

coquettishly, I developed a battery of nervous tics and obsessive-compulsive rituals. These included winking constantly, picking at mites that were not there, and cocking my head side to side three times—it had to be left-right-left, not right-left-right. If I accidentally cocked my head right-left-right, I had to do penance by crawling about with my tail pressed down against the ground so that it would drag behind me instead of standing up perkily, normally, proud and fluffy.

One day, while I was degrading myself thus, wandering aimlessly with my limp tail collecting dust and mud, I happened to glance behind myself (I'd heard a nut fall somewhere in the distance), and a shock wave ran through me—a jolt of energy, a moment of what I call auto-frisson, a hint of at least the possibility of pleasure. The accidental sighting of my dirty, bedraggled tail gave me a glimmer of hope that there was a fuller life to be led.

About the same time, I began wandering away from the neighborhood. You must understand, my family occupied the most sleepy, protected area of the park, acres and acres away from dog runs, paved footpaths, broken glass. I'd heard stories about other places, but only in the form of cautionary tales: little Billy who got lost without a buddy and met some sadistic children with a Swiss Army knife—that kind of thing. But where we lived was far from the reality of the dangerous outer rim of the park. In our enclave, happy families ate together, sang happy songs, and slept long and restful sleeps, dreaming of the delicious nuts they would gather the next day, and the next, and the next. The next area over, down the hill, toward the edge of the field, was where the chipmunks made their home, and though we did not share society with them, we regarded these speedy little fellows with humor and respect. That was my sheltered world . . . until I began my explorations.

Chapter Two. Discovery.
By the summer after I first saw my bedraggled, limp tail, I was taking long perambulations, circling out in wider and wider cir-

cumferences away from home. My father fretted—he'd scratch himself nervously, blinking, and tell me to make sure to start home before the sun was even close to the western ridge. My mother would just sigh and say to him, "Pavel's a big boy now, Piotr, we can't rein him in, he must get this out of his system. He's like my brother, so restless as a youth, but now look, with Sonya and the quadruplets, who would've thought he'd become such a model father."

I let them talk. *Uncle Kristoff with his big belly and thinning whiskers—she compares me to him?* I thought. I cocked my head left-right-left and looked behind myself at my tail. Inside I knew that I was different and that I needed to explore, explore, explore.

I can remember with perfect kinesthetic awareness the feeling—oh, indescribable, flooding feeling—the first time I saw it—the *sight*—a large, steel-mesh basket, full of an array of objects from the world, broken umbrellas, newspapers, deflated rubber balls . . . and more important, also containing napkins saturated with rancid mayonnaise, apple cores, bottles with a little Yoo-Hoo still inside, folded pizza boxes. I stood staring at this monument, knowing I had discovered something important, but not knowing why. In a minute, my question was answered.

I was watching a greasy paper bag which seemed to be shaking in the wind. But there was no wind—my whiskers were perfectly still. I was watching, and wondering, when He emerged in all his glory.

He was dark gray, almost black in places, with sharp, quick eyes and alert, fanlike ears. But best of all, and last to come out of the bag, was his tail—low, sleek, serpentine. The tail I should have been born with. He was what I should have been. What was this otherworldly creature? I was without fear, so enrapt was I with this, the apparition of my true nature, the vision of what I should have seen in a puddle instead of perky brown eyes, little ears, and my obscenely fluffy, baroque tail. I

approached the creature, half disbelieving that a real animal could be so perfect, and asked Him, "What are you?"

He looked over at me, squinting shrewdly. "What do you want?"

"I only want to know what kind of creature you are."

"Rat."

I formed the syllable for the first time, spoke it as an answer to myself, "Rat."

"Yeah. And this is my bin, so you better back off."

I returned to my home in the trees that night feeling hope for the first time. I kissed my mother, scratched Father behind the ear affectionately. It wasn't their fault their son was born the wrong species, I thought. They were innocent little creatures with neither the scope nor the vision to understand the transformation that was beginning inside me.

Chapter Three. Friendship.

For the next three mornings, I woke up early, said a cheery "Bye!" to the folks, and returned as speedily as possible to the rat's garbage bin. I waited there for him, in silence, in shadows, under the cover of a juniper bush. All I wanted was to observe; I did not care, for the moment, if he accepted me or not. He'd slither up from a grate near a narrow footpath, then sidle over to his bin, each paw crossing in front of the last in a lovely demonstration of economy. Every motion fulfilled unanswered questions I'd always silently asked: Why *must* we scamper? Why *must* we eat nuts year in and year out? Why *must* we clean ourselves so often?

His single-minded scavenging was magnificent. The way he found crumbs of muffins, bits of gristle, rawhide shoelaces with a twitch of his finely tuned nose fascinated me. At home, in bed at night, I'd try to twitch my snubby nose in imitation of his sharp one.

Before I continue with my story, let me digress momentarily to share with you some ideas that started to take shape

during those days of Watching and have come to inform my later work. Much has been written about the so-called gaze; we all know that to Look At something or someone is an act of ownership and objectification. However, I put forth that another aspect inherent in all Looking At is a projection into the object, that is, we make ourselves into the Looked At thing, and that is the path of ownership—acquisition through becoming, one might call it. And this acquiring happens only through a losing of parts of the whole original self of the gazer. In some ways, therefore, the one being Looked At, the "Gazee," comes to own the Gazer, as the latter must give up some wholeness in looking (what else, if not this, is the process of seduction?). So for example when I watched the rat, I was becoming him by doing so.

Now I shall return to my story.

There I was, watching, watching, when I felt a tap on my back.

I turned around (glancing out of habit at my bedraggled tail) and found myself looking at a most unusual character: it was feathered and had two wings and two skinny little legs. But up front, where you'd expect a beak, there was a snout formed of gray felt with a little black button sewn on. And behind it, where you'd expect to see just a feathery tail, was attached a long gray piece of yarn. On its head was a sort of headdress, upon which two tiny cardboard ears were fastened.

I backed up further into the shade of the juniper bush, so that I was side to side with the creature. I was obsessed, I hated to be interrupted, but I gathered that if I didn't acknowledge it politely, it might blow my cover.

"May I help you?" I whispered.

"I think I can help you," it chirped quietly, its voice muffled by the felt snout.

I looked it up and down. "How can you help me?"

The creature chirped, "I'm a rat. I've been watching you."

"What do you mean you've been watching me?"

It cocked its head, whistled once, then chirped, "You're a rat too, you just don't know it yet."

I squinted back through the dark green foliage, trying to get a glimpse of my object of obsession. Then I turned to the creature again. "I'm *not* a rat, unfortunately," I said, "and neither are you—you're a two-bit sparrow dressed up like a rat."

"I'm used to hearing that kind of thing," it chirped. "I was accidentally born into this body, feathered and be-beaked, but my soul is a rat's soul, my mind is a rat's mind, and my heart is a rat's heart."

Now, years later, I have to laugh when I think of how I met Donna; then my heart aches from sorrow at what was to be her fate.

"How do you know so much about me?" I asked.

"I know about you because you're like me," she said, "and I remember."

Chapter Four. Coming of Age.

It was a remarkably brief time before I came to accept Donna as a rat almost completely. I rarely remembered she was physically still a bird. We spent all our time together, but I couldn't tell my father and mother about it. They were only grateful that my spirits had perked up. They asked no questions. My perfect sister, on the other hand, seemed annoyed by my cheer. She'd complain about me at the dinner table: "Pavel's not normal."

"He's perfectly fine," my mother would say.

"No he's not, 'cause if he was, he'd want to mate with me when I'm in heat," my sister would say.

"She's right," my father would say, looking worried.

"I'm fine," I'd say, "I just don't like the way she smells."

They decided I was a late bloomer and left it at that.

They were partly right; I *was* a late bloomer, though my awakenings were of an unusual nature. I was blooming into the rat I was . . . and still am in a way.

Donna helped me by shaving my tail down to the gray skin

with a sharp-edged stone from the stream, and she filed my teeth into little points. She taught me "the walk," low to the ground, paw across paw, and "the talk," direct, monosyllabic. At first I wasn't ready to try meeting any biologically born rats. I was happy in myself, and that was plenty.

One afternoon that I remember clearly (bright high sun directly overhead so the meadows were shadowless), we found an unclaimed garbage bin and plundered it. After we'd eaten a stale jelly donut and some baby formula, we lay on our backs looking across the lawn of the park.

And Donna told me the story of how she'd flown away from her mate, Mark, and their nestlings one day, and had found herself at the dump. She was looking at her reflection in an oily pit, despairing that she felt absolutely nothing anymore, when all of a sudden bubbles appeared on the surface. She grew very quiet when she told me this and I prompted her to continue.

"And then what?" I asked.

"Then She emerged," chirped Donna breathlessly, "and I realized . . ."

"Yes, yes!" I exclaimed.

"She wasn't about being sweet and little, she wasn't about dainty sand baths and pretty songs. She wasn't nurturing. She was elemental. And I saw what had always been wrong with my life. I saw what I needed to be. Rat. Raw Power. I am rat."

Chapter Five. Autumn.
Time passed. My sister mated and moved a couple of trees over. My mother was delighted with her grandchildren. To me they seemed dopey and boring, but I was glad everyone else was glad. It was autumn again, and my father was very busy with the nut gathering. My family had learned not to ask questions about the changes in my appearance.

I now knew every inch of the park. I knew every puddle and tuft of grass. Donna would get frustrated—hopping along behind me while I slithered on my belly. It was easier for me to

"be" a rat, and this was an underlying source of tension in our friendship. She'd show off, eating things I couldn't possibly stomach to prove she was truly rat, more rat even than I was.

Once or twice I asked her to show me her flying, but she refused. She said she had completely divorced herself from her bird past, and would make digs at me about how I had to leave my family if I wanted to really be a rat.

On the other hand, I was the one who craved contact with born, biological rats. I wanted to know them, not just observe them. I wanted to hear their thoughts, tell them mine. Donna and I would come across them—a single rat, like my first, guarding a stash of garbage, or a pack of rats—even the young were beautiful and fierce. But Donna was too scared of being laughed at and refused to approach them with me.

I still turn that cold afternoon over and over in my mind, wishing it could have been different, wondering what I could have done.

It was late autumn. All the leaves were off the trees; the air bit at the exposed flesh of my tail. My breath made steam puffs, and my paws were numb on the frosty earth. Donna had backed out many times before, but this time she promised to go through with it: *We would speak to a biological rat* (we never used the word *real,* for we had a tacit understanding of how it would negate our true ratness).

"Please," I had said as we parted the day before, "we'll find one alone, and be straightforward, like the rats we are. We'll ask it if we can have a word with it. Why not try?"

There had been a long pause. "Okay," said Donna, "this time I'll go through with it."

She arrived in a quiet mood; she had slept in a sewer, as usual, but it was getting cold down there. She'd had bad dreams. I remember I noticed that her felt snout needed mending.

We wandered slowly, looking for the perfect rat to meet. We saw a pack of violent-looking young ones, and a pair rutting. Then finally, after hours of searching, toward the western edge

of the park, near the big footpath, I saw the perfect candidate: a little white around the ears, blind in one eye, and the other eye twinkling with sharpness and humor.

"He'll talk to us, I bet he'll like us. Come on," I said to Donna.

We started toward him, and we got a yard away from where he was tugging at a piece of gum embedded in the bark of a tree trunk. He paused and looked at us and started to smile when Donna turned and ran, sobbing.

I stayed my ground. "I'm a rat," I said to him.

"So you are, so you are," he said in a creaky voice.

I was accepted. It was all I wanted. I smiled back at him, and cocked my head—left, right . . . when I heard *it*: a terrible roar and excited, terrified chirping underneath.

"Donna!" I yelled. I turned and ran in the direction of the noise. In a cluster of five bare maples, Donna was running in circles, her two tiny feet clawing at the dirt, while after her came a huge, black beast with bulging eyes. It barked and growled and yelped, and Donna screamed.

"Fly," I shouted. But she kept running on the hard autumn ground.

"Fly, goddamnit, Donna," I yelled. She was tiring, and the dog was gaining on her. In the background I heard someone calling, "Hector, come Hector!"

"Fly, Donna—it's your only hope!" I shouted, even as the dog reached her yarn tail.

And Donna, dear Donna, she turned and looked right at me. "You just don't understand," she said, and collapsed.

A minute or two later, there was the call again, "Hector, puppy, come along!" And from where I hid behind a dead fan-shaped fungus, I watched the dog trot away, licking its lips, feathers sticking to its nostrils and its jowls.

Epilogue.

As I have said in previous, less autobiographical works, defini-tions are prisons; divisions are useful only on the level of great

populations, not on a personal level if one ever hopes to align one's philosophy with the quotidian. I now say, "I am neither squirrel nor rat. Neither dog nor tree. I am nothing, and I am something called Pavel, and what that is I'll never know, and if I ever tell you I know—shake me, shake me hard, for the finality of self-naming is as dull as death.

SUMMER JOB

Between my junior and senior years of college, I had a summer job working at my uncle Marshall's retail business. It was a good deal: the store was located in a small, quaint New England town, and I was given an apartment over his partner Ellwig's garage. The pay wasn't fantastic, but with the free housing, I was saving a fair amount of cash.

The work itself was somewhat tedious. Sometimes an hour would go by with no customers. I'd go around and dust off the magazines and videos with the orange feather duster, or I'd alphabetize the files of back issues, or I'd talk on the phone with distributors, placing orders, listening to them pitch their newest products. Because Uncle Marshall's store was small, we couldn't go nuts with risky new items that might never turn over. Most of the salespeople at these companies were complete bores, with either droning, monotonous voices or wacky, over-enthusiastic ones.

There was one guy, though, at one of the smaller distributors, with whom I struck up sort of a friendship. He was also just working for the summer, also for a relative—his boss was an older cousin, a woman who was in the business for the love of it. The guy's name was Flaherty, and he was a college stu-

dent like me. We were relieved to talk to each other, because we could drop the sales jargon.

"So, um . . . you want the reprinted *Hairless Honeys,* right?" Flaherty would say.

"Yeah, send one or two," I'd say.

"How about that *Teen Twat*? That go yet?"

"No, things have been pretty slow. Marshall says it's the summer doldrums."

Business out of the way, we'd make small talk.

"How's Gert?" Flaherty would ask. He knew I was writing my senior thesis on Gertrude Stein.

"Okay," I'd sigh. I had *The Autobiography of Alice B. Toklas* and *Tender Buttons* on the counter next to the cash register. Something about the monotony of my job made me unable to concentrate on my reading.

"How are the bugs?" I'd ask. He was an entomology student.

"I'm not getting outside with the cicadas as much as I'd like," he'd say. "Eleanor keeps finding little things for me to do . . ."

I knew exactly what he meant. It was good to be able to talk to someone in the same position: the daily drudgery of a specialized business that none of my other friends really cared about or understood. At first, in the beginning of the summer, we'd both thought it might at least be a learning experience. Now, we agreed, it was just a matter of making each day go by painlessly.

It had been about a week since I'd last placed an order with Flaherty, and things had been more dead than ever. No one had come into the store for days except the regulars, Timmy and Bobo. Timmy was one of the town's pets. He was a somewhat "slow" young man, with a soft body and brush cut. His mother was a patient at the state mental health facility, and the townspeople looked out for him. The managers at JC Penney kept him in slacks and sneakers, the kindly waitress at the diner made sure he got fed, and Mr. Crobbar—the barber—trimmed his blond hair once a week. Timmy was an outgoing fellow. He'd stride into the basement shop from the alley, always with his

hand stuck out to shake. I'd have to reach over the counter and have my hand shaken vigorously by his fleshy, cool one. Timmy's thing was boys around the age of eight, maybe nine or ten. He always went straight for the same magazines he'd looked at the day before. He'd pick one out and bring it over, just to show me. He never bought anything.

On this particular day, I'd been dreading Timmy's visit because a magazine he really liked had been destroyed. He'd left it on the counter a couple days earlier. I'd put my iced tea down next to it, then answered the phone. The phone cord had knocked over my drink and soaked *Boy Games* right through. Now I watched Timmy search through his favorite section for that magazine. I didn't want to be the one to teach him a lesson about loss. After flipping through the rack again and again, he came over to me and said, "Where's *Boy Games*?"

I couldn't tell the whole truth. "Oh, Timmy, I'm sorry. Someone bought it."

"Who? Bobo?"

"No, a tourist—y'know, from out of town."

"*Boy Games* is gone?"

"*Boy Games* is gone. I'm sorry," I said.

"*Boy Games* is gone?" he said. This was one reason I tired of Timmy—things often got repeated many times.

"Yes," I said.

"*Boy Games* is gone," he said. He looked down at the carpet. I got off the stool and went over to the racks.

"Here, Timmy," I said. "Look at this—you'll like this one: *Tiny Cornholes*."

"I want *Boy Games*."

"Just take a look at *Tiny Cornholes*," I said. I handed him the magazine. He held it but didn't look at it. I opened it to the middle: a spread of readers' snapshots entitled "Stepson Heaven."

"See, Timmy?" I said. He looked away. "Come on, Timmy, I'll order the new *Boy Games*. Meanwhile, just take this one, okay?"

He glanced at the magazine. "I can have it?"

"Sure, Timmy."

"Thanks," he said. He held it tightly now. He stuck around for another ten or fifteen minutes, talking about the weather and the county fair that would be happening in the big town down the highway. Finally, I reminded him it was lunchtime, and he hurried out to the diner, waving as he left.

I had about an hour between Timmy and Bobo, in which I flipped through the Alice B. Toklas book, underlining every passage I could find that mentioned her mustache. Bobo came in at three, as he always did Tuesdays and Thursdays. Bobo was a neurologist over at the medical center. His specialty was migraine headaches that stemmed from facial tension. He'd developed an operation in which he loosened the nerves of the face and scalp. His area of connoisseurship in Uncle Marshall's shop was socks. He was a short man with salt-and-pepper hair and a beard. He liked to lean one elbow on the counter, his profile facing me, and expound upon the virtues of cotton anklets versus bobby or knee socks. I'd made the mistake early in the summer of asking him what the difference between anklets and bobby socks was. He'd been shocked. "You don't know?" he'd exclaimed. "And you're about to enter your final year of tertiary scholarship?"

I'd looked down, ashamed.

"I just don't know," he said, "what this world is coming to. They teach you all this fancy shmancy postmodern theory and leave out the basics." Then he went into a monologue about sheer woven cotton with a single cuff. That was exquisite, he said, but bobbies—thick, elasticized, opaque, and clumsy. "A different universe, my dear girl," he'd said. "Entirely different."

There were many magazines that featured socks in every issue, but Bobo was a purist. We special-ordered expensive Japanese limited edition folios that were devoted to the white cotton anklet. There was also a Swedish auteur who produced a series of black-and-white films of children with blond bowl-cut hairdos walking through empty rooms wearing nothing but the

anklets that Bobo so loved. That item was underwritten by Swedish public television, and the mail from them was erratic. We'd just gotten in three of these back-ordered videos, so I hoped he'd simply come in, get them, and leave to view them. But instead, he decided to discuss his work with me.

"Woman comes in today," he said, "in so much pain, she can't see straight—her vision goes back and forth between a double image and a tunnel effect."

I nodded.

He continued: "And I asked her when it started, and she said about a month ago. I asked her if anything had changed around the same time—you know, usual stressors: new job, relationship trouble, death in the family. And you know what her answer was?" I shook my head.

"No," he said. "No on all counts. In fact, in many ways, she said, things had been going better. 'Why's that?' I asked her. 'Let's look at that.' You see," Bobo said to me, "being a good physician has a lot to do with an ability to converse with one's patients. 'So, what's changed for the better?' I asked her. And she said, 'Well, I've been losing weight. I'd been really unhappy about my appearance, and then I started a diet in earnest. I've lost fifteen pounds, I met a man who's a cop, and I can wear my high school prom dress again.'

"Now, something was starting to go tick-tick-tick in my head. I asked her which dietary regime she'd been following. And you know what?" he said. I shook my head. "It turned out she was on that new dog biscuit diet. Nutritionally viable, perhaps, but a terror on the jaw. Crunch-crunch-crunch. The human mandible isn't made for such activity. The poor woman, doing something she thought was so beneficial, and creating a whole new problem in the meantime." He gazed off in the direction of the storage closet. I stifled a yawn. "I've seen it over and over again, my girl. So this is what I told her to do: If she's happy with the diet, happy with herself, great. I said, 'Heat up some nice skim or one percent milk to just below boiling—you know, so it doesn't get

that skin—and soak the dog biscuit in that for just a minute, long enough to soften it up. Then eat it, making sure to chew gently. The milk will add calcium,' I pointed out, and I guaranteed her that the headaches would go away. You see," said Bobo, "half these people don't need an operation. They just need a listening ear and some commonsense advice."

I smiled at him and nodded. He'd been in the store for half an hour. "The next person who entered my office—" he began, but just then the phone rang.

I answered. "Marshall and Ellwig's House of Juvenile Erotica—" It was Flaherty. I put my hand over the receiver and said to Bobo, "I'm sorry, I have to take this call."

He said, "See you Thursday," and left with his Swedish product.

"Flaherty," I said, "I'm so glad you called."

"Me too," he said. "I was on the phone with a big deal client in New York, and she kept putting me on hold with that smooth jazz."

I told him about Timmy and Bobo's latest visits. I told him how I felt guilty getting paid to sit around and do nothing. Then I contradicted myself by saying I had to be a darn baby-sitter to Timmy, and that wasn't in my job description. Neither was hearing about craniomandibular disorders.

"Well, I was just supposed to do sales," said Flaherty. "But Eleanor has me looking after Frederick and weeding the garden. I wish I at least had my own place like you. Living with the family is tough."

"Yeah," I said. "But living alone is weird, too. I mean, I've lived in dorms for the last few years. I'm used to eating in a cafeteria. It's an isolated life here. I thought it would be good for my research, but I can't do anything. I mean, what the hell are tender buttons? It's all completely stupid. I'm paralyzed, you know?" Suddenly, I felt tears squeezing their way out of my eyes. I tried to be quiet, but a sob escaped.

"Hey," said Flaherty, "are you crying?" I sobbed again. "Hey,"

he said again, softly. "I was calling because I'm coming to your area this weekend. Eleanor wants me to check out the fairgrounds and figure out where to request a booth."

My sobs stopped. There was silence on the line between us. I'd often wished to meet Flaherty in person, but the reality of it suddenly scared me. I realized I'd been able to be more myself with him, just on the phone, than with any man I'd known face-to-face. There was safety in our abstractness, and now that could change.

"Do you *want* to meet me?" I asked.

"Do you want to meet *me*?" he asked.

There was silence again. Then we both said, "Yes."

Business picked up over the next couple of days because of the various craftspeople and merchants who were in the area to prepare for the fair. One guy, a baseball hat manufacturer, bought all the back issues of *Soft Spots* and *Baby Love*. A woman from Oregon who made vegetarian sandals by hand fell in love with the amateur video selection, and returned every day for three days. "Stuey will love this," she'd say, clutching the videos to her heart. I was glad to be busy. I convinced myself that it was a bad idea to meet my special summer friend. We'd hate each other, he'd think I was ugly, or we'd be attracted and therefore lose that special connection we had just talking. But I knew we had to go through with it, and of course I had secret hopes. My boyfriend at school, Nino, had started to change. He was a philosophy major, and he'd been writing me letters about how every human relationship is based on a power dynamic. *Instinctively,* Nino wrote, *we all want to be dominant.* I'd written him back, *Don't you think it's the great challenge to the human soul to overcome those hierarchical urges?* It seemed like we couldn't agree on anything anymore.

Flaherty was supposed to arrive on Friday, but by closing time there was still no sign of him. I became angry and cynical.

Chicken, I thought. I'm glad I don't have to see him. I straightened up the books and magazines, put videos back in their slots, and went to lock the door.

And there he was: tall, with that shy expression, sandy hair, slightly crooked nose, and horn-rimmed glasses. I opened the door and let him in. He reached out his hand, and I took it, but neither of us shook. We just stood there.

Finally he spoke. "I wanted to come when you'd be alone."

"That's good," I said.

"I stopped in the woods on the way," he said, "and found a tree that was covered in cicadas. The noise was deafening—so high-pitched I could feel the sound beating against my eardrums. I thought I'd do some recordings, jot down some scientific observations. But instead, I just sat down under that tree. The ground was covered in those brown casings, empty husks of the insects. On the leaves and branches, cicada couples clung to each other, mating. In the grass were the ones that had already laid their eggs. These ones were dying, moving slowly, dragging their frayed wings. After seventeen years underground, not singing, not feeling the sun, they come out for that moment, that golden single moment. Then they die."

After that, we were silent. We stood and looked at each other, gazing into each other's eyes. For some reason, I thought of Alice B. Toklas's mustache, which Anita Loos once said was charming and alluring. Then I thought of the love that Gertrude must have felt to pen a full autobiography in the voice of her dear companion. There's that famous Picasso of Gertrude, with the big, asymmetrical almond eyes—not really how her eyes were. Yet maybe that strange skewed expression has to do with Gertrude's capacity for tenderness; perhaps the eyes of love are angled differently than the ones we use to read the paper or cross the street. *Tender Buttons,* I thought. And I finally understood how buttons can be tender.

SUGAR

W hat's in the box?" Mother asked. She was already standing by the closet, holding its door open with her hip. I looked
down at her brown shoes with their spongy soles. I had not
heard her come up the carpeted stairs. "It's her, isn't it,"
Mother said, "it's Sugar." The box was in the closet, on the bottom shelf, next to a pile of folded sweaters. She poked at it
with her foot.

"She'll wake up," I whispered. Actually, she was already
awake. I looked at my shiny black Mary Janes and white cuffed
socks against the pale pink chenille of the bedspread. My shoes
had hard soles, heels with taps on them. I could not come and
go silently.

"Stay right there," said Mother. She backed out of the room,
keeping her eyes on me. She yelled down to Daddy, "Frederick,
we need you up here."

I knew what would happen next. I dropped from the bed
and dashed for the closet. *Sugar's box!* I picked it up and
hugged it. She was starting to move in the box. She had been
asleep for days, and time had passed quietly in the house. Now
I could feel her stretching her limbs, could feel her nails
scratching against the cardboard. There was also the low noise
of bristly fur brushing against itself. I could feel where her

head pressed against the end of the box, and I heard the exhalation of a Sugar yawn.

Mother reappeared in the room. "I told you not to move," she said. I pressed my face against the side of the box and backed into the closet. I felt Sugar's alertness inside the box. She wasn't moving much, but she was listening. I sat down in the corner, between the hems of my winter coat and my long dress. The closet smelled like camphor and cedar. Daddy appeared behind Mother at the closet door. Inside the closet, it was very dark, and the rest of the room was filled with white sunlight: Daddy and Mother were just silhouettes.

Daddy leaned toward the closet. "How's my girl," he said, "my pumpkin? Kitten? Sweet Pea?" I said nothing. "How's my angel? My valentine?"

I whispered, "Fine." Sugar shifted inside the box.

"Why don't you just come out like a good girl and give Daddy the box?" he said. Sugar shifted again.

"She's not going to do it, Frederick," said Mother. "You know how it is."

Sugar knocked against the inside of the box with her head. I squeezed the box tight. A tiny fist punched the wall of the box.

Sugar was fine in my closet.

Every day, I woke up with Mother's eyes on me. She had my school clothes waiting for me. I had seven dresses, one for each day of the week. Plus my long party dress, for the one day each year that Mother and Daddy called my birthday. On this day, they told me I was a year older, and I blew out candles on a cake. The number of candles was always different. One year there might be thirteen candles, and the next, there would be seven.

After I dressed and ate my toast each morning, I would cross the cul-de-sac to go to school. I always turned my head and stared down the long road, a perfectly straight ribbon of pave-

ment with no other houses on it. A deep forest was on the other side of this road, next to the schoolhouse. Something about the density of the trees, whose roots pressed against the low stone wall, always made me linger before Daddy or Mother tugged at my hand and pulled me into the schoolhouse.

Daddy would complain about the expense of educating me, but they agreed it was important to have me properly schooled. Three walls of the schoolhouse were lined with bookshelves, divided into different subjects: math, science, vocabulary, penmanship. On the back wall there was a blackboard. Every day, detailed instructions were left for me in perfect script letters in white chalk on this board. They told which books to take from the shelves, which chapters to read, which words to study. Daddy and Mother would take turns checking in to make sure I was doing the lessons.

Sometimes the vocabulary or math books hinted at something. Words that I could not reconcile stayed with me: *post office, bus, puppy, roller skate, freight train.* I would consider these words and daydream, staring at the dust between the threads of a binding, or looking out the window at the forest behind the schoolhouse. But my work was checked each night, after supper. I could not drift off very long.

While they discussed my notes downstairs, I would go and visit with Sugar in the closet, waking her by whispering her name until she came to silent attention in her box. We would stay like this for three quarters of an hour, listening to each other's wakefulness and breath.

They had taken her away once, but she came back. In the short time since she had returned, she awakened more easily, was noisier and stronger. Daddy and Mother would enter and leave the room silently, inspecting and observing. But now, whenever they approached me, she woke up and listened. Whenever they spoke to me in a certain way, I could feel her moving in the box, sharpening her nails.

I was not supposed to have her in the first place. She came

late at night after a strange evening at the house. It was after dinner, and Daddy and Mother had been checking my notes. I sat at my desk, looking out the window at the endless lawn behind the house. It was an expanse of even green, nothing to see besides grass, no buildings or trees in the distance. I heard voices rise downstairs. Mother and Daddy were arguing. I had never heard them argue. I crept out of my room and stood silently on the landing, and for once, they couldn't hear me over their own noise. They were standing at the dining table. At first, I could only see Mother, but then Daddy's hand appeared and grabbed her wrist. I ran downstairs and into the dining room. I took my mother's other wrist and pulled, trying to get her away from him. She laughed an unfamiliar laugh and shook herself free of Daddy easily. She turned toward me without really looking at me. Then she picked me up and carried me upstairs. It was impossible to move in her arms. She took me to my desk, put me down in the chair forcefully, squeezed my fingers around a pencil, and left the room.

I sat there. I felt my heart beating. I made a tight fist around the pencil, then let go. The pencil dropped, and I watched the blood rush back into my palm.

Later that night, as I lay in bed, thoughts entered my head like transmitted radio signals. I tried not to listen to them, but there they were, speaking, whispering: You are you, you are you, not them, but you. There is more, there is more, there is more than this. You are you, you are you. . . .

I woke up in the middle of the night to the sound of scratching. I had forgotten what had happened earlier and the thoughts that had repeated in my head. I opened my eyes and saw the bluish, moonlit box on my windowsill. The sound was coming from inside it.

• • •

Now Daddy stepped from behind Mother and put his head into the closet. "It's time, Pumpkin," he said. He chucked me under the chin—Sugar banged with a fist inside the box. Daddy tried to chuckle. He slowly reached over to ruffle my hair—then, Bang. Bang. Bang. He jumped back from the closet and stood behind Mother.

"Listen," Mother said. "Isn't it easier to hand the box over than to have it taken away?" Sugar paused, listening. I shook my head and clutched the box. "We don't want to have to do this," said Mother.

Daddy said, "Let's just wait for her to go to sleep again."

"No, Frederick, she's expecting us now. She'll never move from that closet."

They both backed to the corner of the room. They whispered to each other, all the while keeping their eyes on me. Sugar was scraping her nails against the cardboard. Slow, sharpening sounds. I pressed my lips against the bulge in the cardboard where her head was, and its roundness made me feel safe. Mother and Daddy approached the closet again. Their steps were measured. Sugar's scratching paused. We waited. Mother lunged for my arms and Daddy reached for the box, his cuffs rolled down to protect his hands—Bang. Bang. Bang. Bang. Sugar punched and kicked. Daddy dropped the box back into my lap. The punching and kicking got faster. Mother let go of my arms and tried to pick up the box herself, but it was vibrating too intensely. She dropped the box. They moved away from the closet once more and returned to the doorway. Sugar's banging slowed and stopped. We listened to silence.

Mother's voice was different when she spoke again. Low. Soft. Even-toned. "You're going to do a relaxation exercise," she said to me. Sugar and I listened. We had never heard Mother's voice like this before. "I want you to close your eyes," she said, "and imagine you're somewhere very safe."

I tried not to close my eyes, but I found I could not keep them open.

"Imagine you're somewhere very safe," she said again. I imagined I was inside my closet, holding Sugar's box. I imagined she was inside the box, awake but silent, protecting me. "Now," Mother said, "imagine you're in this safe place, and your limbs are getting very heavy. Say to yourself, 'I am going to relax my toes. My toes are relaxing. My toes are relaxed.'"

I imagined myself standing up and walking past Mother and Daddy, who were frozen like statues, not dead but still.

"I'm going to relax my knees. My knees are relaxing. My knees are relaxed."

I imagined myself walking down the stairs, barefoot, making no noise. I imagined myself going to the front door. It was unlocked, and I opened it easily. I stood at the door for a moment, then I stepped onto the lawn. The grass was soft under the soles of my feet.

I'm going to relax my hips. My hips are relaxing. My hips are relaxed. I imagined that I walked across the lawn and got to the edge of the paved road, where I looked down at a gutter clogged with leaves. Then I walked across the cul-de-sac. The rough pavement was hot from the sun.

I am going to relax my shoulders. My shoulders are relaxing. My shoulders are relaxed. The door to the schoolhouse was open, but I walked around the building to the forest.

I am going to relax my neck. My neck is relaxing. My neck is relaxed. There was a low stone wall at the edge of the forest. I stepped up onto it, still carrying Sugar's box. Cool air came from the trees, and there was a damp, growing mushroom smell. The other side of the stone wall dropped further, so I had to climb down backward. Then I turned and walked into the forest. The ground was covered with pine needles. There was a slope to the forest floor, and as I descended, the cul-de-sac disappeared behind me. Soon I found myself next to a brook. I sat on a rock and watched the streaming water split smoothly around twigs and stones. I thought, this would be a good place to let Sugar go, and I took her box over to a safe circle of reeds

growing near the water. I set the box down and walked away from it along the bank. All along the water, red flowers grew and clustered, four or five long stems together, with a spike of color on the end of each stem. The flowers were closed, petals pressing against each other like pods.

I'm going to relax my hands. My hands are relaxing. My hands are relaxed. For a second, I felt something slip through my fingers. I was vaguely aware of a tugging and heard familiar voices coming from a distant place. "I've got it," one of them said. The other said, "Well, take it far away."

I considered the flowers, and a word came to me. Snapdragon. *Snapdragons.* I had seen a picture of them once in a book at school. I bent down and touched a pod of petals. It was firm on the outside, and the petals were closed tight. I squeezed it between two fingers. It snapped open and showed a tender red center. I put a finger in the flower. It was soft now, slightly downy.

I was alone. It was all right. Sugar would come back to me. If she didn't I would go and find her.

AUDITOR

December 17, 1990

This person who called herself my friend said she feared that I was cold and unfeeling. Not that I was really that way, she said, but I seemed to have an iceberg inside of me. She said she was telling me for my own good.

This person who called herself my friend said I needed help with my personality. She said: Wasn't I worried people would think I was not nice? She said: Wasn't I worried I would never find a husband? She said *she* knew there was a lot of good deep down inside me, a goodness and sweetness I just never showed anyone. "I've seen glimpses, you know, moments, where I know you feel things very deeply," she said, "like maybe you feel *so* much *so* deeply you just like shut yourself down to hide from the pain."

But, she said, I *came off* as cruel, yes, she said—she knew it was a defense—but my silence *came off* as catty, dismissive. "Like that girl," she said, "that cashier, just now, you've never seen her before in your life. What has she ever done to you? Why did you have to act like that?"

I shrugged. I thought: This person who calls herself my friend, I hardly know her, either, barely better than I do the stupid, fat cashier at the ice cream shoppe. And obviously, my "friend" hardly knew me. But she followed me around. And

there was my first mistake. I let her trail after me for a while there, for a few weeks. While I was waiting.

If someone wants to be in my presence, that's their business, I told myself. I reminded myself it was better to let her do what she wanted than to do something that might raise her suspicions. But it gets to be too much when someone starts telling you how to better yourself, get help, talk to a professional, or take a class, that kind of nonsense. That night she followed me home, she said she was afraid I might do something terrible to myself someday if I continued living with the iceberg inside me.

She kept talking, all the way back to my house. She was walking a few paces behind me. I was striding ahead of her, not looking, but I could see her arms, waving in my peripheral vision. At one point, she lowered her voice and asked if someone had touched me the wrong way when I was a little girl. I almost spun around and socked her then, but I just continued moving forward, taking bites of my orange sherbet.

She followed me right up the porch steps. She'd been as far as my house before, but never inside. I had never invited her inside.

I just seem to be someone who people like to bother. Why, just recently, during my time in Poughkeepsie, there were several of them: that vitamin salesman with the button that said, "I lost thirty pounds in two months. Ask me how." He told me that he wanted to make love to me. He said I seemed like I needed it. And the woman from UPS who wanted me to come to church with her. Those two I managed to get rid of with simple rudeness. But not so with the person from the Midas franchise on Raymond Avenue.

I'd been in Poughkeepsie for two months when my muffler went. While they put my car up, this person, this receptionist behind a counter, sitting in front of a computer, she smiled and said, "Name?"

"Danita Connell," I said immediately.

"Work phone?"

And I said, "I don't have a work phone."

"Oh, a stay-at-home mom!" she said. "That's what I want to be."

"No," I said.

She was very young. She furrowed her brow, suddenly looking concerned. I found out soon enough that she was pretty new to the job at Midas. She still cared about her customers.

"What *do* you do?" she asked.

Again I answered instantly. "I'm an auditor. An independent, self-employed auditor. I'm based at home."

"Wow. You're new in town, aren't you?" she said, smiling still. She had thin, frosted pink lips; her hair was frizzy from a growing out perm.

I nodded.

"I've lived here my entire life," she said. "Well, really, I grew up in Fishkill. But the area."

I paid, and five minutes later, when I was waiting to make a left turn out of the lot, enjoying the new silence in my car, she ran out and knocked on my window. She kept knocking until I rolled it down.

"You're all alone, aren't you?" she said.

I looked at her but didn't say anything. I had on my sunglasses.

"Know what?" she said. "I want you to see how friendly Poughkeepsie is. Let me show you a nice place after work."

I still said nothing.

"We single gals have to stick together," she said, patting the roof of my car. I should have just driven away. I wish I had driven away. But I didn't.

I was already sick of her, that receptionist thing, when I walked into the bar four hours later.

She had picked the place; it was called Dickens, and it was English-themed, with a bartender in a top hat. Our table was under a plastic structure which, I believe, was supposed to be some kind of gazebo. She ordered a White Russian. I had my usual: club soda. We were there for a total of twenty minutes.

She asked me where I was from, and looking at the Miller Light clock behind the bartender, I said, "Milwaukee."

"Neat," she said. "That's so far away."

I shrugged.

"You must miss your family," she said. I noticed she had started to jiggle her leg under the table. I could hear the sole of her Reebok tapping the floor.

She volunteered, "Like I told you, I'm from Fishkill."

I said nothing.

She giggled and sipped her drink through the cocktail straw.

Later we stood in the parking lot. She cocked her head and gave me a pitying, corners-down smile. She was pink. Her cheeks were blotchy from the White Russian. She wore a flamingo-colored polo shirt with an alligator stitched over one of her wide, flaplike bosoms. She reached for my hand and squeezed it. Her hand was mushy. I pulled my hand away and turned, walking away without saying good night. But she called after me, "Good night, Danita!"

She called me from work the next day. I was lying on the couch, curtains drawn, waiting for the mail to arrive. I shouldn't have picked up the phone. But I admit that I wondered vaguely about her—what kind of person would telephone someone who walked away without saying good night? That was another mistake: answering the phone.

She was calling to say what a nice time she'd had, and let's do it again sometime. Two days later, she was patting my hand with her plump pink one across the table at the brick oven pizzeria.

"You're so mysterious," she said. She slurped from her wineglass. It was her third Chianti. "So tell me, any special guy in your life?"

I looked over her shoulder at the brick oven, that cavern with its arched doorway, logs like tidy sleeping children glowing red inside.

I told her what I told the occasional man who expressed interest in me; I told her what I'd told the vitamin salesman. I told her that my job made it impossible to have relationships. I

couldn't afford to get attached to anyone, not even friends, I said, hoping she'd get the point.

"Oh, you poor thing," she said. "You've been hurt—I can tell—that's why you're scared of intimacy. Don't you think you'd settle down if you met the right man? Someone who treated you like a lady? Wouldn't love change everything? I mean, couldn't you get a job where you didn't have to travel so much? And then," she said, her eyes shiny and wet, her finger tracing the rim of her wineglass, "then I could be your friend."

The cook pushed a pizza pie into the oven with a paddle. I was getting ready to move on anyway. I thought I'd be gone in a couple of days, that I would just disappear before she had a chance to foist herself upon me any further. I knew where my next stop would be—Campbell, Ohio—and my next name, Gloria Freeman, which I had borrowed from an octogenarian Poughkeepsie resident. I always try to find ones who have trouble with their eyes but whose hearing is sharp. I find them in supermarkets, on line at the bank, on park benches. I'm very discreet when I follow them home. Later, I try to sound as kindly and concerned as possible when, standing before a lady like Gloria Freeman, at her front door, I explain that I work for the IRS and I'll need to borrow her driver's license and social security card for an hour. Gloria had been especially friendly and forthcoming—she eagerly gave me her ID and threw in a file folder full of pharmacy receipts and Grand Union coupons.

So by the time that thing and I were having pizza, I was practicing already: Ms. Freeman, Gloria, Glory, Glo Freeman. I already knew my next zip code. But there had been a delay with the trailer I was supposed to move into in Campbell; instead of hitting the road and heading west anyway, the way I should have, I stuck around in Poughkeepsie. That was the second small mistake leading up to the big mistake: I was lazy.

That's how I found myself still in town two weeks after the pizzeria. And that's why it really went wrong with Miss Pink—I couldn't get away from her, and she insisted on fostering our

quote friendship. The colder I was, the ruder I was, the more I pushed her away, the more her desire to change me grew. When she wasn't at the Midas or bothering me, she was, as far as I could tell—not that I cared to think about it very much— watching those television shows where mothers and daughters reconcile, where long-lost twins reunite, where friends confront each other with grievances and then hug and make up. I gathered that some of the ideas she had about telling me how to improve my character came from viewing those programs, where women help each other by tearing each other apart.

It was a bother and a liability to have someone so concerned for me.

That last time after the ice cream parlor, it was just too much. Standing on the porch steps, I found myself blocking out her voice and running through everything I knew about her minuscule, pathetic life: single "gal," father dead, sickly mother in Florida. Lived with a roommate she'd found through an ad in the *Pennysaver*.

I invited her in.

She must have felt encouraged by that, because she marched right through the foyer, down the hall, into the parlor. I followed her. She stood between the painted green bookshelf and the basement door. I didn't turn on the light. She squinted up at me in the shadows.

"I haven't wanted to say this before," she said, "but now that we're here instead of out in public, I think I should. You really don't do enough to make yourself attractive. I mean, *I* think you look great. For your age. But when you don't do anything to cover those little gray hairs or smooth out your complexion, it sends a message to guys. It sends a message that you don't care about yourself. And if you don't care about yourself, who's going to care about you?"

I didn't answer. I reached for the handle on the basement door. I didn't plan this—she had positioned herself there, with

only one thin door between her and a long, steep flight of stairs and the cement floor at the bottom of them. In my head, I assessed her weight, estimated the distance to the base, and calculated the momentum of the projectile.

She stammered, her voice a little higher, "Who's going to care? Who? Who's going to care about you?"

"Let's go into the kitchen," I said, opening the basement door. "Careful, there's a little step up."

Since the day I left Poughkeepsie, I've picked up my pen a hundred times, trying to figure out how and where to begin. I've started scores of notes, then ripped them up—not out of guilt or fear of being caught, but out of a strange sense of embarrassment. Seeing my handwriting made me blush. I never blush. But now I blush again thinking about how close you and I will be when you've finished reading this letter.

I've imagined writing to you for so very long, but I have no idea who you are. I do know you're in a rented trailer at Countryside Estates, on Cooper Road near the border of Campbell, Ohio. You may find this a month after I've moved out, or five years, or ten. I know you must have noticed the place where one of the thin plastic wall panels buckled out of the aluminum runner that should have been holding it perfectly flat. I'm pretty proud of the spot I've picked out for these pieces of paper. Near the floor, behind the fold-down table, next to the kitchen nook.

Confession is supposed to be an act of purification. I have always wondered about those who confess. You see them on television now and then. They look embarrassed and tired, not pure. I'm tired. I'm tired all the time.

This note to you seemed like a practical way to get everything off my chest. As you noticed, I've changed the names of the people involved, and of the places (other than Campbell) where these events occurred. I've tried to put down the story in

a clear, linear fashion. In my professional days, I always had to report on my findings in a clear, linear fashion—so, while I know that I'm not a natural storyteller, I hope that, along the way, I developed some useful skills for expressing myself through the written word. Clear writing is like a logic problem.

I was a logical child. I remember, at eleven, solving problems with my teeth. One side of my mouth was if, the other was then.

Every time I took a math test, I scored 100. I could memorize a sequence of a thousand numbers and repeat them forwards and backwards, arrange them in size order, divide them, add and subtract them—all in my head, without making a single error.

When I grew up, I had a highly paid job as an auditor. I was the youngest female auditor in the country. There was even an article about me in a trade magazine, *Accounting World*. The thrust of the article was my incredible record—the perfection of my calculations, the cleanness of my reports, my superhuman endurance on difficult and complicated audits. The headline said, "Girl Wonder Promoted to Top Drawer." The color picture showed me with my beige sweater, my pocked skin, my hair tucked behind my ears.

I worked for an independent firm traveling from city to city, staying for a month while I made columns of red and black ink, my left hand dancing across the numbered keys of an adding machine. I'd have my own temporary desk in the corner of some office, and although I was so young, and female, I was always treated with respect. I didn't work with a partner the way many auditors did. Everybody trusted that my work would be perfect.

When I was twenty-four, my eyes started going a little. I began to misread numbers. Sometimes I would overlook a decimal point. Or I'd see a six as an eight, or an eight as a zero. I always caught myself, and I would go back and make the necessary corrections. I still had a perfect record.

Then, finally, I made the big mistake. I had known it was coming, I just didn't know when. I still don't know exactly what I did—or didn't do. I had recently been fitted for glasses

but was having a hard time adjusting to them—so maybe it was that. Or jet lag. I was in San Jose. It was a big, high-profile job for my firm, an audit for the second largest computer manufacturer in the country. Of course, it wasn't really San Jose, and it wasn't really a computer company, but let's imagine it was because I can't tell you the real details.

It hadn't been an easy job. The people who worked at the company had been young and intrusive. There was always a partylike atmosphere around the place: I'd seen people snorting cocaine in the ladies' room, and at lunchtime the male employees would put on shorts and play Frisbee. I wanted to be done with the job as quickly as possible. I wrote up my reports in record time and handed in my findings ten days ahead of schedule.

I always sat down at my desk one last time at the end of an audit, to make notes for my own records, notes I would keep with the original handwritten calculations in my ledger book. It was a standard precaution, a backup step that I made grudgingly and halfheartedly.

So there I was, at the end of this irritating job, sitting at my desk with the ledger open in front of me. It was late evening, and I was alone in the office, save the two cleaning ladies, who I heard chatting and laughing as they went up and down the halls emptying wastepaper baskets and recycling bins. I remember taking off my glasses and rubbing my blurry eyes. Then I squinted at the page again. The zeros looked funny; there were too many of them in some places, too few in others.

My stomach turned over. One of the ladies knocked on the door. "No thanks!" I croaked. I went down the lines of the ledger: decimal points wobbled, jumping back and forth instead of lining up in columns the way they should have. Just two zeros and hundreds of thousands of dollars of income had become tens of millions; millions in profit had become billions.

I threw up in a plastic bag left over from lunch.

First I imagined the phone message I would get from my boss: "It's Brian. Call me immediately." I imagined the panic I

would hear in his voice, and the anger, and the betrayal. How he would say, "It's my fault for trusting you."

Then I could see myself in meetings in windowless basement boardrooms, sweating, being forced to apologize, forced to resign.

Then I pictured hearings, with testimonies by my sixth-grade math teacher and my dyslexic older brother. I pictured myself inside a prison cell, with everybody I had ever audited filing past and shaking their heads. "Tsk, tsk, tsk," they were saying.

Yes, I could have told everybody that I had made some mistakes. But instead, I ripped up the ledger and threw the pieces into seven different dumpsters on the way back to my hotel.

When I arrived in my room, the red voice mail light on my phone was blinking. I almost turned around and ran right then. They had found out already, I thought. I could see it all—a conscientious junior accountant (or even an intern) had noticed a discrepancy and had started to dig. I felt dizzy. I threw up again in the toilet. When I came out of the bathroom, there it was still: the strobing red light. Each time it flashed, it accused me. "You. You. You. You," it was saying.

When the phone rang I almost fainted. The whole room seemed to stink from my sweat. Four rings. And then the ringing stopped.

I believed I was trapped. Trapped. I packed and slipped out of the hotel by the stairs. I was in Miami late the next day.

I know. I know. You would have stayed. You would have told yourself: It's a mistake. Everybody makes mistakes. I didn't think that. I didn't tell myself that. I try not to have regrets. I could have done things differently, but I have to live. Don't you agree? Obviously you've done something wrong, too. You must have made a terrible mistake as well. After all, you live in a trailer outside Campbell, Ohio.

• • •

At eight A.M. my last morning in Poughkeepsie, just as I was zipping up my duffel bag, the doorbell rang.

I froze.

I was heading to Campbell, Ohio. I could sleep in my car until the trailer was ready. Since the night before, everything had changed. I could no longer wait.

The doorbell rang again.

I crept over to the window and peeked out, hoping for a Jehovah's Witness or even the return of the UPS lady. But there was an unfamiliar Hyundai parked in front of the house. A man stepped off the porch and into my line of sight. Short, slight beer belly, khaki pants. He looked around, shielding his eyes from the sun with his hand. Baby face, blond.

I collected myself. I had to go downstairs. My car was parked in the driveway; I was obviously home. He didn't look like the law.

"Yes?" I said through the screen door.

"Um, Miss Connell? I'm Tyler? I'm looking for Corinne?" he said. (They were those kinds of names, names like Tyler and Corinne.)

"Corinne?"

"Yeah." His voice got a little stronger. "Corinne. My fiancée. Petite. Wavy hair."

Gloria Freeman, I thought. Glory, Glo. Daughter of Freeman. Good old Freeman. My daddy. I pictured Campbell, that red dot on the road atlas where I would soon be safe.

I opened the door just enough to squeeze through. It closed behind me with a snap.

"Oh, *Corinne,*" I said. I squinted to see inside his car. Nobody. I looked up and down the block. Nobody.

"She didn't come home yesterday after work," he said. "She never came home."

She had told me her roommate's name was Mamie. Now I remembered her laughing nervously and volunteering that she didn't know much about Mamie's past. She lied to me, I

thought, and I found myself shaking my head. For a moment I wished I could go on one of her TV programs and confront her: *Why didn't you tell me about Tyler?* I imagined myself screaming. *What was the point?* And I imagined her sobbing, *I thought you wouldn't want to be my friend.*

I noticed that I was still shaking my head. I had to say something, so I said, "That's odd." I forced myself to put something like a smile on my face. I ached under my arms as my sweat glands puckered and wept.

"I know you're her friend," Tyler said, glancing down and to the right as if he could see through the piece of plywood I had hastily nailed across the basement window at three A.M. "She talks about you all the time . . ." Suddenly he relaxed and smiled a strained smile. "And I'm sure she talks about me all the time to you. I hope you don't think she's a pain in the ass. She means well."

"Oh, I'm sure she does," I said. I sounded terrified and sarcastic at the same time.

"Can I sit down?" he asked, nodding at the porch steps.

"Be my guest," I said. I realized that I had started to tremble, huge shivers running up and down my whole body. I pulled my cardigan tight across my chest.

"I guess she's kind of like my mom," he said, then half-winked at me. "Don't ever tell Corinne I said that. Deal?" I nodded. I wondered if he would ever leave. I pictured him moving into the house. I pictured him getting in my car and talking all the way to Campbell.

"I bet Corinne's told you all about Mom. I mean, Mom can be kind of nosy, kind of a busybody, but even though she annoys the hell out of me, I always remind myself that Mom has a heart of gold. Okay, for example, she'll come into our place and look at everything, pick up the pieces of mail, the dirty dishes, whatever, and comment on them. But what am I going to do, tell her not to come over? Tell her to call before she comes? You can't do that to your mom, right?"

I leaned against the wooden column under the sagging eave.

"Thing is," he said, making himself comfortable on the top step, "as you know, we're getting married next month, and, well, tell you the truth, I've been a little worried about how much time she's spending with you. She may have told you we've been fighting some."

I nodded. In the rear of the basement, the cement floor ended, and there was a five-foot strip of dirt floor, which became moist and spongy every time it rained.

"Nothing serious, not big fights—just—I don't know—she's always going 'My single friend this, my single friend that.' I was starting to think you were a bad influence. I thought that you were out partying together, maybe flirting with guys, that kind of thing . . . but now that I'm meeting you"—he looked at me with pity—"I can tell that wasn't the case."

I looked at my fingernails, the reddish brown dirt under them. I had done the best I could with the shovel, considering I had been in a hurry.

He cleared his throat. I tucked my hands into the pockets of my pants.

"She feels sorry for you," Tyler said.

"Uh-huh," I mumbled.

"Sometimes she says she feels sorry for me. She says I'm a big baby. Maybe all guys are, what do you think?"

"I don't know . . ." I said, thinking about his neck—it was thick, but not muscular. The flesh looked soft and pliant. What would the difference be? I thought. I pictured two mounds next to each other, mounds as plump and neat as the people inside them. Then my stomach turned over, saliva spouted into my mouth, I thought I would throw up.

He stood again, hiking up his pants. "Well, sorry to bother you. Maybe she went to TGIF with her mom and sis, and crashed on Mamie's sofa. She does that once in a while." He laughed and winked. "Especially when she's mad at me. Man, I

can't wait until this whole wedding thing is out of the way."

We stood there for a few seconds, facing each other. I realized I had to say something. "Well, good luck."

"Thanks a bunch," he said, reaching out his hand. He waited. I had no choice: from my pocket, I pulled my scared and sorrowful hand, with its stained nails and sore muscles. I offered it to him. He took it. He pumped it up and down. "I feel so much better now that we've talked," he said.

After I watched him drive away, I went back inside the house. I had rented it only semifurnished, and had never added a single chair or rug. I walked into the living room, where the shades were drawn as always, and I sat down on the tattered love seat in the corner. I knew that every moment I spent dawdling was a wasted one, a risky one, a dangerous one. Yet I couldn't move. I found myself thinking about the love seat. Closing my eyes, I could picture the people who had sat on it before I moved in— I imagined couples: entwined lovers; husbands and wives watching television; newlyweds giving each other backrubs; young parents, bickering from exhaustion after putting an infant to sleep. I thought about Corinne and Tyler, "Corinne" and "Tyler," how they must have nestled, snuggled, pressed their soft bellies together under the covers in some condo in Wappingers Falls, between the mall and the IBM compound. I could see her small, frizzy head moving over his groin. I could see him, shaving cream on half his face, catching her awkward breast in his hand as she stepped out of the shower.

He would never find her.

It was very hard at first when I got to Campbell. I didn't know how I would live, what I would do with myself. I kept my ear to the radio, my eyes on the seven-inch black-and-white TV. But I guess that the news about what happened in Poughkeepsie never made it that far. I spent a long stretch living in this trailer, longer than I'd been in one place for years. I cut my hair,

• • •

dyed it black. I started wearing dark nail polish. When my nails were bare, I could still see traces of dirt between them and the tender part of my fingertips. I was polite to all of my neighbors.

As I said, I try not to have regrets, but I do sometimes find myself looking back on my finest moment as an auditor. I wish you could have seen me at my best. I wish you had known me then. I had pride, I really did. I was on top of the world.

I was twenty-two, and coming to the end of a grueling stint at a PepsiCo satellite office in Spokane. It was a monthlong job that turned into six weeks. I was working down to the wire. It was midnight on the last night of the audit, and I had uncovered proof of what the corporate headquarters had suspected: that large sums of PepsiCo money allotted for supplies, petty cash, and promotions had been reabsorbed and recorded as earnings, and that the Spokane office was actually losing money instead of turning a healthy profit. I was making my way through the records of the last quarter when there was a knock at the door. It was the vice president who ran the satellite. He was wearing a sweat suit, and his velour jacket was zipped up tightly across his blubbery middle. He asked me how it was going, and I told him it was going well, and that I was just about done. He came closer to me and put his hairy hands on the edge of the desk. I kept working. After a little while, he said he guessed it wasn't looking too good for him, and I shook my head. The next thing I knew, he was down on his knees on the carpet, his jaw trembling.

"Please," he said, "please, this is going to kill me. Do you have to do this? Does it have to be so bad?"

I looked at him for a second—the greasy sweat on his temples, the tiny bald spot I'd never noticed when he was standing up.

"Isn't there anything we can do to make you stop?" he said.

I sharpened my red pencil.

See Through

The first man says to me, "I missed you."

I say, "I missed you, too."

He says, "How was your weekend?"

I say, "Fine, fine. I went to a barbecue."

He says, "I'm having trouble hearing you."

I move the microphone. "Is that better?"

"Yeah. That's great. You look nice."

"Thanks," I say. I smooth my hair. "How's your girlfriend?"

"She's okay. I don't know. Let's talk about you."

"What do you want to talk about?" I ask.

"Tell me about the barbecue," he says.

"Well, it was in San Rafael. I took a bus there."

"A bus! Baby I woulda drove you."

I laugh. "I had spareribs."

"You're no vegetarian, no sir," he says. "My girlfriend makes wicked carne asada."

"So now you *want* to talk about her?" I say.

"No, no, baby. Forget about her. Tell me something . . ."

"Something what?" I watch my reflection in the glass. My eyebrows raise to look inquisitive.

"Aw, you know, baby doll . . ." He takes off his hat. It has a fire extinguisher over the visor. He is a fire extinguisher repairman.

"You know how I like it." A clunking noise, and he digs in his pocket for another quarter. The sound goes out until he drops it in the slot. "You *know*. Pretend I'm your man. Tell me what you're gonna do to me tonight when I get home from work."

"I'm going to lie you down on the blue velvet couch . . ."

"We got rid of that couch," he says.

"What kind of couch, then?" I say.

"Flowered. A sofa bed, so her mother can come and visit."

"Okay, I'm going to lie you down on the flowered sofa bed . . ."

"No—not there," he says. "That's where her mother sleeps."

"Okay, where, then?"

"The deck, out back," he says.

"The deck," I say. "I'm going to take your hand and lead you out to the deck. I'm going to be a little bit forceful."

"Not too forceful," he says.

"Of course not, honey," I say. "I'm going to lie you down on the plastic deck chair. . . ."

"Hey, you know what?" he says. "It's a full moon tonight."

The quarter drops, and there is silence again until he puts another in the slot. I stare over his head at my reflection.

"So you lie me down in the deck chair," he says, "and I'm looking up at the moon and you open my belt, and I can feel your fingernails on my legs." I drag my fingernails lightly across the glass in front of him. He is unzipping his pants. "Do it, okay?" he says.

I reach over to the hidden little shelf and take down the latex phallus. I shut my eyes. He once said to me, "You know, that's not nice, a girl keeping her eyes open when she's doing you." I put it in my mouth. I listen to his breath, trying to pay attention to his rhythm. The regular dropping of coins punctuates his quiet, polite panting. I open my eyes after I hear his customary gasp and sigh. I smile at him. He smiles at me as he zips up his pants and puts his cap back on.

"Really," he says.

"What," I say.

"If I was really me, and you was really you," he says, "would you? Like if you just met me at a party or something, would you?"

"Of course," I say. "See you soon."

The second man says to me, "I've never done this before."

My mike is still off. I sigh before I turn it on.

"Well, you're very cute," I say. And he *is* okay, a young man with long blond hair, wearing a Metallica T-shirt. He isn't used to the glass. He squints at me.

"I'll do whatever you command," I tell him.

"Is your name really Sheena?" he says.

"Absolutely," I say.

"My sister has a kitten named Sheena," he says.

"Where are you from?" I say.

"Marin. San Rafael."

"Oh, I was there last weekend for a barbecue," I say.

"Like, you go to barbecues?" He sounds disappointed.

"Well, orgy sort of barbecues," I say. "You have nice arms. You must be a drummer." I see my face in the glass, watch my lips pucker around the word 'drummer.'

He grins and nods. Then he says, "You have nice tits." He turns red, looks behind himself, and leans forward. "Is it okay to say that?"

The quarter drops, but he is prepared. He has a little sack of them from the front counter, where they charge one-twenty-five for four quarters.

"Of course it's okay to say that," I say when the sound buzzes on again. "Actually, I'm flattered, and I'm getting a little hot."

He pushes his hair behind his ear and says, "Like, you *are*?"

"Ooh, yeah," I say. "It's not every day that someone like you picks my booth."

"Well, I saw that picture of you outside, the one in the blue

bikini." He looks at me. "But you're not wearing a bikini now."

I make a show out of wiggling my slip over my head. "Better?" I say. I'm making my voice as high and breathy as I can and still remain audible. I sit in my bra and underpants.

"Like, *yuh,*" he says. He stares at me leaning toward the glass. He just looks me up and down. His breath makes a spot of steam.

"You look a little like the girl in the Coors Light ads," he says. I giggle. "But she's thinner," he adds.

"Well, you know they airbrush the hell out of those pictures," I tell him.

"No, don't get me wrong," he says, "I'm, like, totally into you. You're gorgeous the way you are."

"Well," I say, "you are too."

He says, "I also like your legs, but not as much as your tits."

"Thank you." I spread my legs a little bit. It's always like this the first time: a cataloging of body parts.

"Could you, like, turn around?" he asks me.

"For you, baby, anything." I turn around and look over my shoulder at him. He is slipping another quarter into the slot.

"You also have a nice enough ass," he says. Then he whispers, "Kind of like my sister."

"The one with Sheena?" I sit back down.

"Uh-huh," he says. "She plays tennis. She's the pro at the Strawberry Point Country Club."

"Ah. Do you work out?" I ask him. "You look awfully strong."

"No. Just drums and I do landscaping. I help with the golf course at the club."

I start to feel I'm losing him. He may have satisfied his curiosity enough. He could get up and walk out. I've heard people say I don't work hard enough to keep the customers in my booth. And last week I was out with a cold. I can't afford to have him leave.

I look him in the eye and whisper into the mike, "You know, it's always been a fantasy of mine to make love on a golf course."

"Really? No *way*!"

"Yeah, I've always wanted to lie down in the grass, that really soft green grass, and have a hunky . . . dude . . . give it to me."

"Well, like, if you want to come to the club sometime, we could go there at night and stuff," he says.

"No, I can't wait, let's pretend right here, okay?" I say.

"Okay." He's nodding. He's catching on. I go slowly, take him through step by step. He asks if he can call me Tiffany. He isn't embarrassed to touch himself after I assure him he has a cute dick. I wiggle a lot. He seems to like that.

On my lunch break, I go to the dressing room in the basement to use the pay phone. A couple of the other girls are down there, but none of them talk to me anymore. A few weeks after I started this job, a nine-dollar lipstick fell out of my bag. One of the girls picked it up and raised her eyebrows. I told her I'd shoplifted it from Walgreens, but she just shook her head. For a while after that, they all seemed curious.

"Are you in college?" one girl asked me.

"No," I said. "I dropped out. For now." She looked down and sucked air in through her teeth.

A couple of them asked where my family was. "The East Coast," I'd answer. I didn't want to be specific. More stares, a shrug.

"You got any kids?" asked a small woman who had her twins' school pictures taped inside her locker. "No," I said, adding, "but maybe someday."

Then, one night in the dressing room, I was taking off my makeup when they all gathered around me. To this day, I have no idea if they planned it or if it just happened spontaneously, a natural culmination of the tension that had been building for weeks. One of them stepped forward and said, "So, what are you doing here anyway?"

I looked around at them. I tried to figure out how to answer, but wound up just standing there with my mouth half open. They turned away from me, looking sideways at each other with disgusted smiles. Since then, it's been the silent treatment. Still, I'd rather use the phone here than out on Market Street with its crackheads and Women Against Pornography. I dial Bill's number and reach his answering machine, a tape of him playing his talking drum—the rhythmic gulping sound, and his hands slapping its taut skin. I hang up without leaving a message.

A couple of years ago, soon after we met, Bill started to complain that his life lacked spirituality. I was working at a 970 number then, and sometimes he'd call and pay to talk to me. We'd chuckle as I spoke to him as Cherise or Maria. Then, out of the blue, he decided that he would start his own religion. He announced it to me one morning while we were waiting to order coffee and scones. He told the woman on line behind us, and the guy behind the counter, too, while our milk was being steamed.

Bill threw himself into his project: he wrote prayers and designated holidays and sacred symbols. He found a secluded spot in Golden Gate Park, and made a shrine there out of branches and rocks, velvet and novena candles. "I finally have something to believe in," he'd tell me, sighing, every night before he fell asleep. "I'm at peace for the first time in my life." In the near-dark, his eyes looked shiny and serious. I'd smile at him, and then he'd kiss me and pull me close.

About a year after Bill came up with his idea, someone told Channel 2 about his shrine and they did a news feature on him. As soon as he saw himself on television, he stopped believing. But the next time he visited his spot in the park, he was surprised to find some people waiting there for him. So he has to show up and worship. His fans expect him to be there at certain times, he says. He can't let people know he has lost faith.

Yesterday was the first day I was out and about after my

cold. I got up with Bill and walked with him to the park. On the path, right outside the spot where he has his shrine, I kissed him. I put my tongue as far back as I could and mashed my lips against his. But I was thinking that I needed to get nail polish on the way to work. The ridges on the roof of his mouth felt hard like fish bones. After I ended the kiss, I said, "Have a good day, baby."

"Don't talk to me like that," he said, turning and walking away.

"What do you mean?" I said, following him.

"You know, that *voice*."

We stepped into the clearing. There were a few kids with pierced lips standing around, waiting to see Bill worship. One of them held a video camera.

"But that's my voice."

"No it's not, Liz," he said. "It's dirty."

"But you like being dirty, baby," I said.

"That's exactly what I mean." He stamped his bare foot. "That *baby* shit."

I looked over at his audience. A girl clicked a steel ball rooted in her tongue against her teeth. She stared at me. I knew she wanted me to leave.

"I'm sorry." I lowered my voice. "I can change the way I talk. How do you want me to talk?"

Bill shook his head. "I just don't buy you anymore," he said to me, loud enough for everyone to hear. He turned to face the spectators, inhaled deeply, and rolled his eyes back into his head. Then he kneeled down in the grass and started lighting candles.

The third man sits down with his face in the shadows. "Bitch," he says. He has an older voice, high-pitched and restrained like Mr. Rogers. "Dirty bitch." I can see the sleeve of an egg yolk–yellow cardigan when he puts the quarter in.

"What do you want, sir?" I ask. I lean forward.

"Get back, whore," he says quietly.

I try to work with it. I say, "I've been very bad. I need to be punished."

"Shut your dirty trap," he says.

I watch myself in the glass, sitting still, waiting. I hold my breath and try to be very quiet. Once, I read that the gaze holds power, that by looking at something you come to own it. I've also heard it said about names: if you call something by its true name, it belongs to you. I stare into my own unblinking eyes.

When I was a girl, I got a baby doll whose eyes closed when she lay down. I was scared for her, and pulled out her tiny plastic eyelids, so she could always see. Her eyes were blue, transparent, frozen. I would sit her on the bed across from me and we would look at each other in silence.

The quarter falls. I see the yellow sleeve moving in the dark.

ABOUT THE AUTHOR

Nelly Reifler has published stories in magazines such as *Bomb, Black Book, Post Road, Exquisite Corpse,* and *The Florida Review* as well as the anthologies *110 Stories: New York Writes After September 11* and *Lost Tribe: Jewish Fiction from the Edge.* A graduate of Hampshire College and of Sarah Lawrence College's writing program, she received the Henfield Prize for two of the stories in this collection. Her plays have been performed in the United States and Australia, and she currently teaches at Sarah Lawrence College. She lives in Brooklyn.